LOIS LENSKI

HOUSEBOAT GIRL

Other Books by Lois Lenski

Historical

PHEBE FAIRCHILD, HER BOOK
A-GOING TO THE WESTWARD
BOUND GIRL OF COBBLE HILL
OCEAN-BORN MARY
INDIAN CAPTIVE
BLUEBERRY CORNERS
PURITAN ADVENTURE

Regional

BAYOU SUZETTE
STRAWBERRY GIRL
BLUE RIDGE BILLY
JUDY'S JOURNEY
BOOM TOWN BOY
COTTON IN MY SACK
TEXAS TOMBOY
PRAIRIE SCHOOL
MAMA HATTIE'S GIRL
CORN-FARM BOY
SAN FRANCISCO BOY
FLOOD FRIDAY
HOUSEBOAT GIRL
COAL CAMP GIRL
SHOO-FLY GIRL

HOUSEBOAT GIRL

By **LOIS LENSKI**

J. B. Lippincott Company
Philadelphia and
New York

1957

For

my beloved

river children

DEFINITIONS

chute—a channel at the side of a river, or a narrow waterway between an island and the shore.

johnboat—a square-ended, flat-bottomed river skiff, propelled by either oars or an outboard motor, well-adapted to use on slow-moving rivers and sheltered lakes.

revetment—a river bank paved with asphalt to prevent erosion.

seine—a large net, one edge provided with sinkers and the other with floats.

stage plank—a long board from a houseboat to the shore—a gangplank.

towhead—a low alluvial island or shoal in a river with clusters of cottonwood trees.

CONTENTS

FOREWORD

A river is an invitation. Since the beginning of time, it has always drawn men to its waters.

To the great Mississippi and its tributaries, they have come for many reasons—to explore it as conquest, to find a market for their products, for cheap and convenient transportation, or for pure love of the river itself. The pull of the river is a mighty one and has attracted all sorts and conditions of men—explorers, raft and keelboatmen, steamboat and packet boatmen, deckhands and sea captains, wanderers, adventuresome sportsmen, criminals and gamblers. Fugitives from the law gave the river people a bad name at a time when many river towns were outside the reach of the law. Fortunately, with better policing of our waterways at present, the river is no longer a convenient hideout for lawbreakers.

Last but not least, the river has always attracted the family man, who makes his living from the river itself. He traveled—and still travels—in a floating house, drifting lazily on the current or using motorboats to shove in and out of tight places. He usually sells his houseboat down river, and if he returns to the north, uses other means of transportation.

The "shantyboater" takes with him his wife and children, his cats, dogs and chickens, his fish boxes, boats, nets and fishing gear. He is a simple but colorful type, a man of character and courage. He knows the pull of the river, he meets its challenge for he is no weakling, and his love for it is so great that he is never happy to be away from it for long.

Such a man is Henry Story. He and his wife, Lou Story, are river people "by birth, ancestry and inclination" and have brought up their children, Peggy, Irene, Pete and Debbie, on the river between Paducah and Memphis, having made fifteen or more trips between these two places. When Harlan Hubbard drifted down the Mississippi River in 1949, he met them in their houseboat in Nonconnah Creek below Memphis, and he told of this meeting in his book Shantyboat. *Through Mr. Hubbard's introduction and with his help, I was able to locate the Story family at O'Donald Bend, near Luxora, Arkansas, in the summer of*

FOREWORD

1954. They were in a newer and larger houseboat than the one at Nonconnah Creek, the children had grown, were as much at home on the river as ever, and I found them a perfect "story family."

For a period of six weeks I stayed in Luxora and was able to see them almost daily on their houseboat. I ate meals with the family, went out on the river with the children in their johnboats, took notes and made many sketches, helped to sell fish to the cotton pickers, and learned by firsthand experience all the intricacies of trotline and hoop-net fishing. Not the least of my pleasure in this family was learning and sharing their river philosophy and sensing their happiness and satisfaction in the river as a way of life. By contrast with the increasing commercialization, conventionalism and standardization of our average American way of living, theirs seemed to offer a singularly fresh and wholesome approach, a nearness to the world of nature, and a sense of true freedom and independence of spirit not quite possible on land. I learned not only to know the Story family, but to love and admire them as well.

With a few exceptions, life on the river since the days of Mark Twain has been ignored in literature to its great loss. The river is as much an environment as mountain, prairie, plain, swamp or woodland. It controls the life of the people who travel on it and of those who live on its banks and of all those who love it because they have "the river in their blood." A fine river tradition has grown up to enrich our American heritage, and it is as alive today as it was yesterday, for it is being preserved for us by those rugged wholesome people who have deliberately preferred it and its vagaries to any other way of life, even though its monetary rewards are negligible. To them goes my highest admiration and regard.

It has been a privilege and a rare pleasure to write of the river people and to tell how they live for the benefit of the many who do not know them. The river children have been ignored and neglected, even though they live dramatic, vivid, if not dangerous lives. I have found them daring and courageous, resourceful and independent, poor perhaps in this world's goods, but sweet, lovable and good.

To the Henry Story family and to Harlan and Anna Hubbard, and to my many friends in Luxora and Osceola, Arkansas, go my sincere thanks for the help they gave me in making this book possible.

Lois Lenski

Lutean Shores,
Tarpon Springs, Florida
February 1, 1957

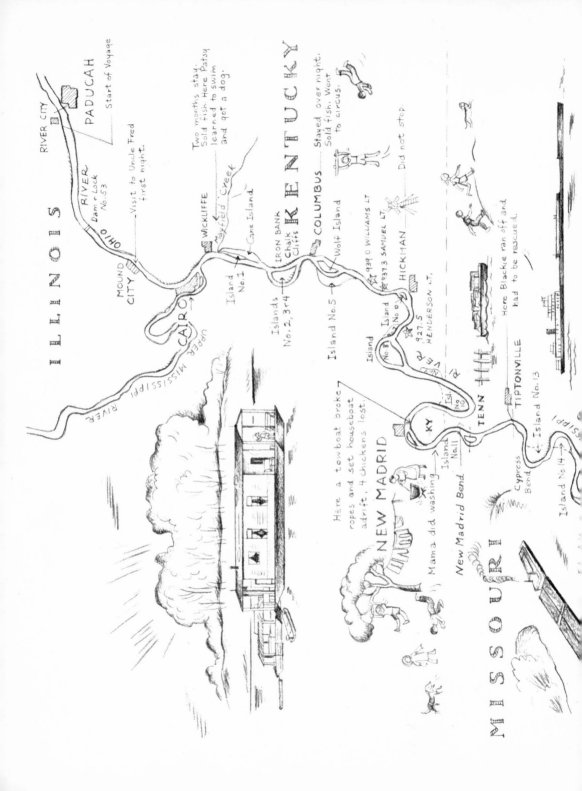

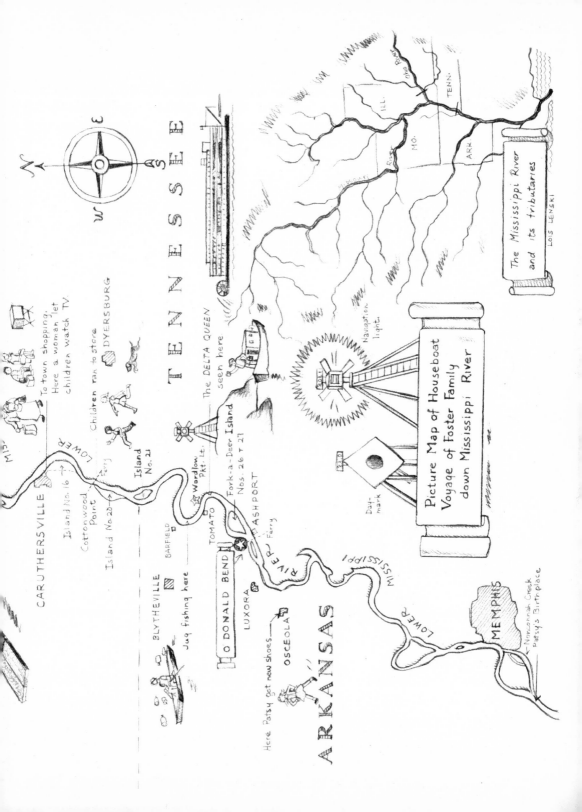

Picture Map of Houseboat
Voyage of Foster Family
down Mississippi River

The Mississippi River
and its tributaries

LOIS LENSKI

MY HOUSE IS A BOAT

Song of the River Children

Words by Lois Lenski

Music by Clyde Robert Bulla

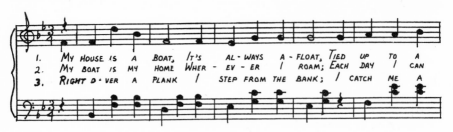

4. The big waves may splash,
The waters may dash,
My boat it rides high,
Inside I keep dry—
Let the sleepy old river run by!

Copyright 1957 by Lois Lenski and Clyde Robert Bulla

HOUSEBOAT GIRL

CHAPTER I

River Calling

The house was nearly empty now. The rooms looked strange and bare. Patsy picked up a box of dishes and took it out on the porch. She was a pretty girl with soft brown eyes, and blond hair falling loose on her shoulders. She wore a skimpy cotton dress and a red sweater.

"Is Mama coming?" she asked.

Patsy stood at the top of the steps and looked. The house and porch were raised high off the ground on six-foot posts, so she had a good view. Across Front Street and beyond the wide weedy stretch of the river bank, she could see Daddy's new houseboat. It was floating in the water at the river's edge. The river was the

Ohio, and across on the other side, she could see the shoreline of Kentucky. It was May and the river was low.

Daddy had started building the houseboat on the bank in April. He bought the hull, a large heavy barge, from a man up river. Then he set the framework on it and closed it in. He said it was going to be the biggest and best houseboat of all. Just a little shove from Old Garrety's bulldozer had been enough. The houseboat slid down the slick peeled willow poles on which it had been resting, right into the water. Due to the falling river and the slackening current, Daddy was anxious to leave.

The people who drove along Ferry Street or Front Street stopped to look. They were very curious and Patsy got tired of their questions.

"What's it for?" they asked. "Buildin' Noah's Ark?" or "You gonna put it in the river and go somewhere?" When Daddy told them the Foster family was going down river, they thought he was crazy. But Patsy knew he wasn't.

Patsy remembered Daddy's last houseboat. She was all excited over the new one until the boys and girls at school began to tease her. They started calling her *shanty girl* and *river rat*. They said, "Don't fall in and drown yourself!" and "Watch out! A garfish will bite you!"

But school was out now and Patsy was glad. Both she and her older sister Milly had passed but Dan was held back. He had to do the second grade over again. Little Bunny was only five, still a baby. She had never been to school at all.

It took a month and one day to build the houseboat. Now it was done and the Fosters were moving in. They were moving all

[2]

the furniture out of their house on Front Street and putting it in the houseboat. As if a houseboat could ever be a home!

Patsy could see Mama now, coming back up the dirt river road in Uncle Ed's car. Mama was taking all the small stuff herself—the clothing, cooking utensils, curtains, dishes and other things. Daddy had borrowed a truck to haul the stove and beds and heavy furniture. It was surprising how much the houseboat could hold. Milly was down there helping to get everything in order.

Mama came in the kitchen to get the pots and pans. She was a plump woman, with loose dark hair, dark eyes and a pleasant smile. She wore a cotton dress and a flowered apron. Patsy followed at her heels. She heard voices out the window and ran to look. There were the Cramer girls and Ginny Cobb coming over.

Mama climbed on a chair and started taking things out of the

cupboard. "Here! Take this," she said, handing one thing down after another. Patsy put the pans and jars and canned goods into boxes and baskets.

"Patsy! Patsy!" called the girls outside.

"You can't go now," said Mama. "You stay here and help me. This is my last load. If I can take everything, we can eat on the houseboat tonight."

Patsy frowned. She felt almost like crying. She did not like this moving business.

"Why do we have to go on the river?" she asked. "Why can't we be like other people and take our summer vacation here?"

"You'll like it on the houseboat once we get settled," said Mama.

"But the Cramers and the Cobbs don't go on the river," said Patsy. "Mrs. Cobb said people don't live in houseboats any more the way they used to."

"Your Daddy likes living on the river," said Mama. "He's not happy anywhere else."

"But *I* like living in town," said Patsy.

"You'll like the river, too," said Mama with a smile. "How about going swimming every day?"

"I can't swim," said Patsy.

"It's time you learned," said Mama. "Milly will teach you."

"Patsy! Patsy!" called the girls again. She could hear them giggling beneath the kitchen window.

A cat came walking into the kitchen. It sniffed in cracks and corners.

"There's Aggie's cat," said Mama. "Chase it out. Aggie ought

[4]

to feed it so it would stay home."

"Can't I take it with me on the trip?" asked Patsy. "I'd catch fish every day and feed it."

"Pushcart Aggie wouldn't thank you for stealing her cat," said Mama.

"She's got six parakeets," said Patsy. "She'd not even miss it."

Just around the corner by the alley stood an old bus used as a house trailer. It had dishpans and pots of blooming flowers on its hood, a moon vine growing up over the door and two tanks of bottled gas on the left side. This was the home of old Aggie Stiles and her son. She was called Pushcart Aggie because she pushed a cart and picked up junk to sell. All the river children knew her well. She kept her birds in a cage indoors. She loved her cat and scolded the children if they threw stones at it or pulled its tail.

"Patsy! Patsy!" called Ginny Cobb.

The girls were waiting on the front steps when Patsy went out.

"Are you really goin' down river and never comin' back?" they asked.

"Of course we're comin' back," said Patsy.

"Then why don't you leave your furniture here?" asked Alice Cramer. "Why you movin' everything out?"

"We need furniture on the houseboat," said Patsy. "We'll cook and eat and sleep there. How can we do it without furniture?"

But Alice's question disturbed her. In her own short life of nine years, Patsy had already lived on four houseboats. This was the fifteenth houseboat her father had built. They had all gone down river and stayed there. Not one of them had come up river again.

"When you comin' back to River City?" asked Ginny.

Patsy hung her head. "I don't know," she said in a low voice.

The girls could not guess how sad she felt inside. They kept on talking excitedly.

"Boy, it must be nice to go sailing in a houseboat," said Alice. "You goin' all the way to New Orleans?"

"I wish *my* daddy would build a houseboat," said Faye.

"We helped your daddy build it, didn't we?" said Ginny.

"Remember when the storm came and blew it over?" said Alice.

"Yes," said Patsy. "My daddy got his leg hurt when the boards came down on top of him. He got a man to help him put the frame back up. That time he made it so strong he says the wind can never blow it down again."

"We carried boards and put them where he told us to," said Faye.

"We swept it from one end to the other, me and Patsy," said Ginny.

Patsy put her arms around her friends, happy in the warmth of their love. They walked around to the back yard.

Mrs. Foster loaded the car and drove to the houseboat. Soon the girls came too, carrying a chicken coop. Several of Patsy's chickens were poking their heads out between the slats.

"What are you bringing the chickens for?" asked Mrs. Foster. "I told Uncle Ed he could have them."

"Oh no, he can't," said Patsy. "Daddy told me to take them

[6]

along. They're my pets and I've named them all. There's Old Red, Fluffy Tail, Mrs. Fuzzy, Shoo-Fly, Mrs. Cackle, Jenny Brown, Stiff Legs and Fuss-Box."

Daddy came up in the johnboat—a rowboat with square ends. He was a tall, wiry man with a thin, weathered face. He wore overalls and a blue shirt and cap. He looked so much like young Abraham Lincoln, he went by the nickname of Big Abe. Patsy's brother Dan was often called Little Abe.

Daddy turned to Mama.

"Can't turn a girl loose from everything," he said. "Let her keep her pets. There's room for the coop on the cabin boat."

"Well, I hope the stupid hens won't fall in the river and get drowned," said Mama. "When they start laying, we'll have fresh eggs to eat. And a roast chicken will make a nice change from fish."

"You can have the eggs," said Patsy, "but you can't eat my hens, and they're not stupid. I'm going to train them to go up and down the stage plank."

"That girl's strictly a tamer," said Daddy. "She'll train those hens and teach 'em tricks. She can tame a jaybird up on a limb by just lookin' at it! I never knew anyone like her."

On the afternoon before departure, the neighbor women came to see Mama. "See our outfit?" Mama pointed.

The houseboat was tied to an overhanging willow. On the other side of the tree, Daddy's cabin boat and fish barge were also tied up, ready for the voyage tomorrow. The cabin boat, sometimes called the "push boat," was not a boat that could be lived on. It was a heavy barge with a crude cabin over the engine, and it had square ends. It was to be used at the stern of the houseboat for pushing. It could also pull the houseboat by a towline. There were also two johnboats, one to use as a rowboat and one with an outboard motor, and a smaller motorboat.

"Can't see why you're leavin'," said Mrs. Miller. "Mussel shellin's good here in the spring."

"It's too hard on a man's back," said Mrs. Foster.

"I hated to see this houseboat go in the river," said Mrs. Cobb.

"As long as it was on the bank, I knew you folks were still here," said Mrs. Cramer. "Now it's in the water, you'll soon be gone."

"Abe can stand a house just so long," said Mrs. Foster. "Then that old river starts callin' and gives him no peace."

"Won't your kids fall in and get drownded?" asked Mrs. Cobb.

"Abe says they're as safe on water as on land," said Mrs. Foster, "and as safe in deep water as in shallow. He says more people drown in their own bathtubs than in the river!"

The women talked a while, then one by one went back up the river bank to their homes. Uncle Ed came to take his car, but had to wait until Mama made one last trip to the house.

"I like to forgot my wire clothesline and props," said Mama. "Don't know how I could do the family wash without them." When she returned, she brought her curtain stretchers, too.

Patsy couldn't bear to let the girls go. "Milly's goin' to teach me to swim this summer," she told them.

"In the river?" cried Faye Cramer. "I'd be afraid of the garfish. They'll bite your legs off!"

"Once when I went out fishin' with my daddy," said Ginny Cobb, "the garfish came right up by our boat. They were as long as the boat was. They bit the end of our oars."

"Old Garrety and his wife they like 'em," said Lora Bragg. "She fries 'em and they eat 'em."

"Ugh!" said Janey Miller. "I bet they taste terrible."

"I'll tell you why Faye hates 'em so," said Alice. "A garfish bit her once. She put her finger in the water and a mean old garfish bit it."

"I'm not afraid of a garfish," said Patsy. "I had one in a tub for a pet once. Don't you remember?"

"Oh, you! You'd keep *any*thing for a pet!" Lora laughed.

Patsy asked the girls to come and see the houseboat. They came and she showed them around.

"Gee! Now that it's all furnished, it's just like a house," said Ginny Cobb.

[9]

"Sure! Why not?" asked Patsy.

It was like a house, an oblong box set on the hull in the middle, leaving open porches at each end. Inside there were three rooms. The first was the living room, with a cot in the corner for Dan. The next was the bedroom, with a double bed for Mama and Daddy, and a bunk bed for the girls. Milly slept on top, and Patsy below, and Bunny on a little cot. The third room was the kitchen, with Mama's bottled-gas stove for cooking, a cast-iron wood stove for heating and the large dining table. There were cupboards on the wall with rims on the shelves to keep the dishes from falling off.

Mama came back and started hanging flowered curtains on the little windows over the sink. Patsy pulled a chain from a light bulb in the ceiling, but the light did not flash on.

"You even got electric lights?" asked Alice.

"Sure," said Patsy, "only it's not connected now, because we're leavin' tomorrow."

"And a gas stove?" asked Faye.

"Sure," said Patsy. "We got two bottles of gas." She pointed out on the back porch.

"And running water?" asked Ginny, looking at the sink.

"No," said Mrs. Foster, "only from the river. We'll have to carry our drinking water."

"Well, I think it's just as good as a house," said Ginny.

The girls went out on the tiny back porch.

"Why, look!" cried Faye. "That's Paducah right over there. Look how close we are."

"Paducah! That's nothin'," said Patsy. "Soon I'll be seein'

Cairo and Memphis and Vicksburg and New Orleans. Remember all those cities we studied about in geography?"

A wide stretch of placid water, the great Ohio River, reached across to the other bank. In the channel over on the Kentucky side, a towboat with a long string of barges was passing, headed down river.

"Look!" said Alice. "I bet this houseboat will go faster than that towboat and get to New Orleans quicker."

"Yes," said Patsy. "We'll go fast all right. We'll just float along on the current. We won't need any pushin'."

A long freight train came across the river from Kentucky on the railroad bridge high overhead. It made a deafening noise and threw a cloud of black smoke down into the river valley. The girls could not talk until it had passed.

"Come on!" cried Patsy. "Let's play tag. Try and catch me!"

Narrow walks called *guards* on the two sides of the houseboat connected front and back porches. Patsy ran round to the front porch, the girls at her heels. Round and round they ran, but Patsy was too fast to be caught.

"Girls!" called Mrs. Foster out the window, "do be careful. Don't be runnin' around on the guards all the time. If you fall in, the river won't stop for you, it'll carry you on where it's goin'. Not one of you knows how to swim and I don't either, so I can't pull you out."

She spoke too late. Suddenly there was a great splash. Mrs. Foster looked out. There was Ginny Cobb in the river, splashing wildly and screaming at the top of her voice.

"Hush up, Ginny!" called Mrs. Foster. "You're not drowned.

[11]

The water's only up to your knees."

"I'll save you, Ginny," called Patsy.

Patsy found an oar and held it out to Ginny. The other girls took hold and they all pulled. Soon they brought the dripping Ginny up on the porch.

"My mother will have a fit," said Ginny. She and the other girls ran up the river bank, and Patsy went with them, even though she heard her mother say, "Supper's ready." The rest of the family sat down to eat without her. It began to grow dark.

"Where's that girl gone?" asked Mama. "Abe, you'll have to go look for her."

"No need," said Daddy. "Here she comes now."

With hair flying, Patsy came running down the hill and over

the stage plank. She carried something in her arms, but she did not come into the kitchen. She stopped in the bedroom.

"What's that you've got?" asked Milly. "Mama, she's hiding something under the bed covers." The children came in to look. "It's moving," said Dan.

Meow! Meow! a faint cry could be heard.

"Patsy, *where* have you been?" asked Mama sternly.

"I . . . I went . . ." the girl was still out of breath. "I wanted to say good-bye to the girls . . ."

"*Where* have you been?" asked Mama again.

"I wanted . . . to say good-bye to Aggie . . ." Patsy began.

"Is that her cat?" asked Mama. "Did you steal it?"

Milly threw the bedcover back and a small cat appeared. It was black with a white throat. It had three black feet and one white one. It meowed again. Patsy picked it up and hugged it.

"No, Mama, honest," said Patsy. "Aggie gave it to me . . . for a going-away present."

"Patsy!" cried Mama. "Is that Aggie's cat?"

Daddy spoke up. "Let her keep it. She's got to have her pets."

"But if it's Aggie's cat?"

Little Abe settled the matter. "It's not that old cat of Aggie's. It's one of the kittens. Aggie was trying to give them away."

"All right then," said Mama.

Patsy looked up with her most bewitching smile. "She really *did* give it to me . . . to keep."

"Four kids on a boat is enough without a cat," said Mama.

"Let her keep it," said Daddy.

Patsy smiled and hugged the kitten close.

[13]

CHAPTER II

Down the River

Patsy woke up early the next morning and wondered where she was. Then she remembered. They had slept on the houseboat. The motor in Daddy's cabin boat was roaring loudly. The cabin boat was pushing the stern of the houseboat. Daddy was getting ready to go.

Patsy jumped out of her bunk. She ran to the porch in her pajamas. Bunny and Dan were still in bed, fast asleep. The roar of the motor stopped. It was still dark.

The river was as quiet and peaceful as a lake. Nothing was stirring, not a single bird, not a leaf on a tree. A dawn hush was over everything. Only a glow of pink showed in the east.

Again the loud roar of the cabin boat motor broke the stillness.

"Come, Patsy," called Mama. "Come and eat breakfast."

Patsy smelled bacon and went to the kitchen. Mama and Daddy and Milly had eaten. Milly liked to think she was grown up. She was out in the cabin boat with Daddy, helping. She always said she had to work like a boy.

It seemed strange to be eating down below the river bank. Above the slope of weeds and grass, Patsy could just barely see the tops of her house and of the others on Front Street. Were the Cramers and the Cobbs getting up now, too? Was Pushcart Aggie eating breakfast or feeding her birds? Would Ginny and Faye soon come flying down the hill to say good-bye? Mama brought bacon and egg and set it down before her. But Patsy could not eat. She tried a biscuit and it nearly choked her. She pushed back her chair and went in the bedroom to dress. When Mama called her, she said, "I'm not hungry."

Then before she knew it, they were out in the river. Daddy had let go the lines and pushed off.

"This is some outfit we've got!" Mama stood on the porch with her hands on her hips. "A fish barge, a cabin boat, a house-boat, a small motor boat and two john-boats. People will think there's a towboat coming!" But Patsy did not listen.

Why didn't the girls come? Weren't they up yet? Didn't they want to say good-bye? Didn't they know she was going down the river? Even Mama didn't care. She was clearing up the breakfast dishes just as if they were still in their old house on Front Street. Nobody cared but Patsy.

The girl stood on the little porch and looked back. The river

[15]

breeze blew her blond hair off her shoulders, and there was sadness in her eyes. She watched the tops of the houses until they disappeared. Then the houseboat went round a bend and the little town of River City, Illinois, was gone. Patsy slumped to the floor and leaned back against the wall. She held the black kitten in her lap and patted it.

"You feelin' sick?" asked Mama.

"No," said Patsy. "I'm all right."

Mama went away and left her.

The river world was different. The minute you got out on the river, the high banks flattened out. The river was a world of water with a low shoreline on both sides. All familiar landmarks disappeared. The houseboat went under the high railroad bridge and soon it, too, was gone. It crossed over to the channel on the Kentucky side. The river was so wide here it was like being on the ocean. Now they were cut loose from the bank for good.

It was different from being in a boat, because now they had their home right with them. When you went out in a boat, you could always come back to your home on the river bank. But in a houseboat, you took your home with you, so there was no coming back. It was two years since they had lived in Daddy's last houseboat, but Patsy remembered just how it was. She remembered the one before that, too.

Patsy Foster was a river girl. She was born in the middle of the Mississippi River. Mama often told her that. Mama told her so often she got tired of hearing it. She liked the river—of course she liked the river. The river and fish and floods and rain and mud were a part of her life. Everybody who lived on the river

[16]

liked it. Daddy always said that once you had a drink of river water, you could never get away from the river. Patsy liked many things about the river, but she didn't want to live on it all her life. She liked a house in town, too.

The worst thing about the river was that it was always calling you, always taking you away from the friends you made in town. You had to like it whether you wanted to or not. That was the bad thing about a river. Sooner or later it got a hold on you. Patsy made up her mind she was going to hate it this time.

"Oh! Oh! Come and look, Patsy!"

Bunny and Dan were up now. They were on the front porch calling.

"Here comes a big tow!" cried Bunny.

"Here comes a towboat with fifty barges!" called Dan.

Patsy walked slowly round on the guard till she came to the front porch.

"I've seen towboats before," she said, dropping down on the leather couch. The couch was an old auto seat that Daddy had rescued from a wrecked car. She cuddled the black cat in her arms.

"It's only got twelve barges, Dan," said Patsy. "Can't you count yet?"

Milly stood out front and signaled to her daddy behind in the cabin boat. But he had already seen the towboat coming before it gave two toots of its whistle. First came the oil barges, four rows of three abreast, then the towboat which was pushing them up river. The houseboat could not get too far away without leaving the channel.

The deckhands all came to look. They acted as if they had never seen a houseboat before. They called and waved and the children waved back.

"Well, boys," called Mama, "how do you like this stylish outfit of ours?"

"Where you goin'?" called Dan. "Stop and take me with you."

"What you cookin'?" called Milly. "I smell something good."

"They holler just as if they know us," said Patsy, "but I couldn't hear what they were saying."

Patsy thought of the friends she had left behind. What friends could a girl make on the river? Only the deckhands on a passing towboat who waved and shouted and then were gone. Deckhands who would never be seen again!

"When those big tows come along, it worries me," said Mama, "because I don't swim and I know Daddy couldn't save all of us."

"Who's fallin' in?" Milly laughed. "Remember *I* can swim, too."

Milly went around in shirt and jeans like a boy, except for the earrings in her ears. She tied her hair back with a string, except when she curled it. She liked to boss the younger children.

"Watch out, kids!" she called. "The waves are coming."

Abe Foster was ready. He steered the houseboat at an angle, to meet the oncoming waves. Up and down rocked the houseboat, while the children staggered about, trying to keep their balance. Loud thumps could be heard indoors, followed by cries from Mama. A lamp slid off a shelf and some dishes fell. A chair was knocked over.

Then the towboat, moving swiftly, passed around a bend and was gone.

Suddenly a hen began to cackle close at hand. Patsy jumped up. Her chickens! She had forgotten all about them. She ran quickly and jumped over to the cabin boat. She fed and watered her pets and talked to them for a while. She promised them a run on the river bank whenever Daddy tied up for the night.

She came back and slumped on the couch again. Bunny and Dan started a game of jacks on the floor. The houseboat had straight going now for seven miles. The river was wide and flowed northwest to the Joppa lights.

Patsy felt tired and lazy, for there was nothing to do. No games to play, no place to go. No friends to see—nobody but her own family. She was cut off from everything and everybody. She watched the clouds floating by overhead. Now and then she saw a bird on the wing. Then she must have dozed off to sleep. After a time she was roused by Dan's shouts.

"The locks! We're coming to the dam and the locks!"

This must be Lock and Dam No. 53 above Olmstead. That meant they had passed Joppa already. The river was very wide here. There were mussel beds between Joppa and Grand Chain, and a good many mussel diggers were out. Their boats, with brails hung close with hooked lines, were scattered out over the river, outside the channel.

Mama came out on the porch and sat down. She took Bunny on her lap.

"No more shell digging for Daddy," she said. "I'm glad of that."

"But how will he make money then?" asked Patsy. "To buy food for us to eat and clothes to wear?"

"Don't you worry," said Mama. "Your daddy's the best fisherman on the Ohio and Mississippi rivers! We'll make out all right."

Then Milly was out front pointing and shouting to Daddy back in the cabin boat. They were coming close to the locks. Patsy jumped up to see. Going through the locks was exciting.

The gates had already been opened. Patsy heard the lock men shouting to Daddy. They told him how many feet the drop to the lower level would be. It was a long slow process getting Daddy's outfit in and the gates closed behind. Then the drop began. Daddy's motor was shut off, and it was very quiet in the lock chamber. Down they went, with the walls rising higher and

[20]

higher on both sides. It was like going down in an elevator.

"Oh, boy! This is fun!" cried Patsy.

But Bunny got scared. She ran indoors and hid under Mama's bed, crying. Patsy went to coax her out, but she would not come.

Then at last, outside, the lower gates began to open, and they could see the lower level of the river ahead. Daddy started his motor and began pushing the houseboat out through the gates.

"Come on out, Bunny," coaxed Patsy. "We're through the locks now."

Bunny came and hid her face in Mama's apron. "I couldn't see anything under the bed," she said.

"Under the bed is a good safe place to hide." Mama patted the little girl on the back. "I don't like the locks, either," she said.

After the lock excitement there was nothing much to see. The banks on both sides were low and far away. There were no towns on the Kentucky side from Paducah all the way to the Mississippi River.

The day wore slowly on. A Diesel towboat, hauling coal from West Virginia, caught up with the houseboat and went on ahead. Mama cooked dinner and then Bunny and Dan took naps. Patsy got tired of the kitten, found Dan's harmonica and played for a while. Mama took up a batch of mending. Milly came in, complaining of a headache.

Patsy decided to go fishing. She climbed up on the houseboat roof and brought down a pole and line. She baited her hook with a piece of fat. Then she sat down on the porch floor and threw out her line. But nothing happened. No fish came to bite. All at once her fish pole fell out of her hand into the water. It floated

[21]

beside the hull. Patsy held onto the porch post with her hand, leaned out and stretched her leg out over the water toward the pole.

"Oh Patsy! *Don't!*" called Mama. "Don't do that!"

But the girl had already caught the fish pole between her bare toes and was hauling it up on deck.

"What's the matter?" she asked her mother.

"Oh, you make me so nervous," said Mama. "Looks as if you're just determined to fall in!"

"Are there no fish at all in this old river?" asked Patsy.

"Too many dams on the Ohio and too little current," said Mama. "Wait till we get to the Mississippi. It's plumb full of catfish and scale fish, too."

"When will we get there?" asked Patsy. To her surprise, she found a large jumping fish on her line.

"Tomorrow maybe," said Mama.

"Where are we going to stay tonight?" asked Patsy.

"At Mound City," said Mama. "We'll go visit Uncle Fred this evenin'. Can't pass by with Uncle Fred lookin' for us."

The sun was already setting when the Fosters reached Mound City, Illinois, a real river town with an active boatways on the water front. Daddy tied up in a small cove to one side. He came in the kitchen to wash the oil and grease off his hands and face, and to change his clothes.

The minute the boat stopped, the children rushed to the bank. It seemed good to be on land again. "You'd think they'd just crossed the ocean," said Mama.

Patsy put a plank from the cabin boat to the bank. She shooed her chickens out of their coops and up on land. But it was getting dark and they did not want to go. So she sprinkled corn on the plank to coax them back in again. They seemed to know that the coop was their home. They did not like the strange river bank.

Then Uncle Fred was there with his loud booming voice. He took all the Fosters in his car to his house up in town. They ate supper at Uncle Fred's, played games for an hour with the cousins, and then Uncle Fred brought them back again.

Already the houseboat had begun to seem like home. Soon they were all asleep in their beds, Tom, the cat, curled up at Patsy's feet. The river water lapped lazily around the hull and the moon rose over the wide expanse of the Ohio River. All was peace and quiet in the Foster houseboat.

The next morning Patsy was up early. She put on a T-shirt and blue jeans and went out to the cabin boat. She talked to Daddy while he tinkered with the motor.

"It won't take long to get to Cairo," said Daddy. "Then we'll be on the Mississippi."

"That's a mean old river, I guess," said Patsy.

"Everybody says so," answered Daddy with a laugh, "but it's not so bad when you know it. There are plenty of things to cause trouble—wind, pile dikes, tricky currents, snags and sand bars. And there's nothing worse than meeting a tow in a tight bend. The trouble with that old river is, it wiggles too much!"

Patsy laughed. She felt safe with Daddy.

Daddy could not read a book, because he had never been to school. But he could "read" the river like a book. Born in Kentucky, he had lived on the river all his life. He knew every bend and sand bar and buoy and navigation light. He knew what every riffle, eddy or "slick" meant before he came to it. He knew all the crossings without need of the buoys and he never used a map.

"Will we stop at Cairo, Daddy?" asked Patsy.

"We might go to the Boat Store," said Daddy. "I need more rope and other supplies."

Suddenly Patsy heard a motorboat coming. Around the bend a man appeared in an outboard johnboat. Above the sound of the motor, his loud whistling could be heard. Daddy stopped work and looked up.

"Well, I'll be jiggered!" he said. "If that's not Whistling Dick, I'll jump in the river. I'd know his whistling a mile off."

The next minute the two men were shaking hands. The man was not a stranger at all, but an old friend of the Fosters. He had a cheerful smile and wore his britches with the legs rolled up. He patted Patsy on the back and came over to the houseboat for breakfast. Mama was glad to see him, too.

"Dick, you're a part of the scenery," said Mama. "Every time we go up or down the river, we see you somewhere."

"And this is Little Abe," said Whistling Dick. "A chip off the old block, I can see."

"Are you the man that never stops whistling?" asked Dan.

Whistling Dick laughed. "Yes, Little Abe," he said, "my whistle never runs dry. When I get tired of whistling, I sing." He started singing *Pop Goes the Weasel* in a loud voice.

Dan began to march around the table, trying to whistle the tune.

"Are you fixin' to go shelling, Dick?" asked Abe Foster.

"Yep," said Whistling Dick. "I been on the Cumberland all

winter. Got my houseboat beached up there. But the river will soon be gettin' low and there's no fish left in it. So in the summer I always come over to Illinois. I got me a little cabin back up here on the river bank, with a cooking vat and some brails and hooks. I'll soon be selling mussel shells."

"You can have 'em all, and the pearls, too," said Abe Foster. "I'm tired of that job. Luggin' them heavy shells up the river bank like to broke my back. We're off down river now on a summer vacation. There's still plenty of catfish left in the Mississippi!"

"Watch out, catfish!" cried Whistling Dick. "Big Abe Foster's coming!"

The men began to brag about their big hauls of fish. Patsy wondered who was the better fisherman, her father or Whistling Dick. Soon he said he had to be going. Patsy held the cat in her arms as she watched him get in his boat. She waved good-bye and could hear his cheery whistle long after he was out of sight.

"Daddy says we might stop at Cairo," said Patsy.

"Good!" said Milly. "We'll go uptown and do some shopping. I want to get me a pair of high-heeled shoes."

"High heels?" Mama laughed. "On the river you'll all go barefoot."

Soon the houseboat was in the river again. Now there was something to look forward to—the big city of Cairo. Everybody called it Ka-ro, not Ki-ro like the capital of Egypt. It seemed a long time since the Fosters had left River City, a long time since Patsy had left her friends. She had other things to think about now.

As they neared the city, there was more traffic on the river—

[26]

dredges and towboats and barges and motorboats. Soon the sky was darkened by city smoke and ahead lay the railroad bridge across the Ohio. There were two other highway bridges out from Cairo, one from Illinois to Kentucky and the other from Illinois to Missouri.

"Is this Cairo?" asked Patsy. "I don't see any town. I thought it was a great big city."

"It's big enough," said Mama, "back up behind that wall. It's bigger than River City, but not as big as Memphis."

The city was circled by a concrete flood wall that rose up from the river like the ramparts of a walled town. Cairo's location was a dangerous one, locked between two mighty rivers. With the Ohio on one side and the Mississippi on the other, the city had had to protect itself from innumerable floods and annual high water. Hence the great sea wall built of concrete.

Abe Foster came to a place where there was a sloping rock wall, which might have been a former steamboat landing. He edged the houseboat in and tied up. Milly had on her good dress, ready to go to town. But Daddy said no, there wasn't time. The sky had become cloudy and he was afraid of rough weather ahead.

"I'll get my rope and supplies at the Boat Store and be right back," he said. "I want to get down to Wickliffe early. There's a good harbor at the mouth of Mayfield Creek."

"Buy us a book of river maps," said Mama.

"Who wants a map?" asked Daddy. "I can't read it."

"Well, I can," said Mama, "and I like to know where we're going."

Milly took off her good dress, disappointed. When Daddy came back with the rope, he brought the big yellow book of Lower Mississippi River Maps, put out by the United States Army Engineers. He tossed it into Mama's lap, and Mama got out her glasses to look at it. Patsy looked, too. Map No. 1 showed Mound City and Cairo. Patsy followed their day's course with her finger. She found Wickliffe and Mayfield Creek a few miles below.

Soon the houseboat was moving again, drifting lazily on the current, no power needed. The clouds had lifted a little and the river was still placid. The Fosters passed by a group of shanty-boats, some beached in a grove of cottonwoods and others afloat along the river bank. They came to Cairo Point, where towboats and dozens of barges were tied up. Cairo Point was a towboat terminal. Here barges of coal, grain and minerals were transferred to other routes for continued hauls up or down the Mississippi, Missouri, Illinois or Ohio rivers.

"Where does the Ohio River end and the Mississippi begin?" asked Patsy. "How can you tell?"

"The water from the Missouri is yellow and muddy," said Mama. "It brings a lot of mud with it and dumps it into the Mississippi above St. Louis. The Missouri has always been called the Big Muddy. The Ohio just flows gently into the Mississippi, then gradually the water gets muddier and the current swifter, and you know you are in the Mississippi."

The sky grew cloudy again, and they began to notice the change. The river was no longer the placid Ohio. Driftwood sailed past on a speedier current. The wind began to blow up choppy waves. Daddy stayed in the cabin boat behind, controlling the course of the houseboat. He had to steer carefully along the dangerous Wickliffe shore.

Mama and Patsy kept on studying the river map. Patsy saw that all the islands were numbered, starting at Cairo and going south.

"I'm going to count all the islands as we go along," she said.

"That'll be a hard job," said Mama. "Many of them are missing, some are washed away or joined to the mainland. The river keeps changing its banks all the time, but the state lines never change."

Daddy seemed to know where he was going without looking at a map. Before long he nosed the boat into a little cove at the mouth of Mayfield Creek, below Wickliffe. Just in time, too. The lines were all made fast and Daddy was washing up on the back porch, when the downpour came. It made a heavy tattoo on the flat tar-paper roof of the houseboat.

Mama had a pot of coffee on the stove and had started supper. She fixed baked pork and beans, mashed potatoes and iced tea. The houseboat rocked on the waves, but it was snug and cozy inside. It felt just like home.

Mayfield Creek

"But I thought we'd keep going," said Patsy, "and not stop till we got to New Orleans."

Mama laughed. "Nobody said anything like that."

"And here all we did was to cross the river over to Kentucky," the girl went on.

"You never can tell what you'll do on the river," said Mama. "That's why Daddy likes it so much. It's a free life—he can do what he pleases. He's his own boss. If he wants to go, he goes. If he wants to stay, he stays."

"But if he likes the river so much, why doesn't he stay on it?" asked Patsy.

"Stop fussing," said Mama. "There's good fishing here and we're staying until Daddy feels like moving on."

"Oh—I just want to see New Orleans *so bad!*" cried Patsy.

"Go and feed your chickens," said Mama.

A month had passed and the Fosters were still at Mayfield Creek. It was a pleasant location in the chute between Island No. 1 and Cane Island, with a sloping river bank and trees for shade. They lived in the houseboat, fished up and down the river, and peddled the fish in nearby towns. Daddy had rented a second-hand Ford to drive around in.

"We might as well have stayed at River City," said Patsy. "Daddy fished and sold fish there. He had his own little fish house and all the people in town came to buy from him."

"There were three other fish houses in River City," said Mama. "Daddy had too much competition."

Fish, fish, fish! The Fosters' whole life was nothing but fish. Sometimes Patsy wished she had never seen one. She never ate fish and she hated the constant fishy smell.

One morning Mama was washing clothes on the river bank. Daddy had strung the wire clothesline up between two trees. When Mama began to hang the clothes up, she looked at the sky.

"I hope it won't rain," she said. "Bring the clothespins here, Patsy."

Patsy heard voices and looked up.

"Mama," she said, "somebody's comin' to see us."

A woman came down the river bank. She held two children by the hand, a boy of eight and a girl of ten.

"Howdy! How you folks doin'?" she called out.

Mrs. Foster said politely, "Good morning."

"I'm Miz Preston," the woman said. "I live in that two-story house up there on the road."

"Glad to meet you," said Mrs. Foster. She hung up the last pair of overalls and came over. "Come in and set down." To Patsy she said, "Go get the clothes props and prop up the line."

The woman followed but stopped at the stage plank.

"I seen your shack down here . . ." she began.

"My what?" asked Mrs. Foster.

"Your shack!" repeated Mrs. Preston. "Oh well, what do you call it, then?"

"I call it a houseboat," said Mrs. Foster.

Patsy came up and stared at the newcomers. She had seen the children up by their house but had never spoken to them. They

were nicely dressed and had socks and shoes on. Their hair was all slicked back. They stared back at her in return.

"On the Ohio River, it's called a shantyboat," explained Mrs. Foster, "but in Louisiana and Arkansas it's a houseboat."

"Do you *live* on it?" asked Mrs. Preston.

"We sure do," said Mrs. Foster. "Come on in, the stage plank will hold you. Come on in and set down."

The women and children stepped across the plank warily.

"Aren't you afraid your kids will get drownded?" Mrs. Preston asked.

"They're too mean for that!" Mrs. Foster laughed.

Patsy spoke up. "We're not either mean."

"Well, Patsy is O. K.," Mrs. Foster admitted. Tom the cat was rubbing against her skirts. "But between her and the cat, I don't know which one is meanest!"

"Don't she ever fall in?" asked the woman.

"Laws yes," said Mrs. Foster. "Patsy's my unluckiest one. She's *always* fallin' in the river."

"I never let my two go near it," said Mrs. Preston. "I don't trust that old river as far as I can see it." She held her children firmly by the hand.

Patsy looked at them in disgust. They were worse babies than Bunny and Dan. There would be no fun playing with them.

Mrs. Foster laughed. She and Mrs. Preston sat down on the leather couch.

"Fallin' in is an old story with us," Mrs. Foster went on. "That's why I'm gettin' gray hairs. Milly—she's my oldest— learned how to swim at Memphis when she was four. She'd fall in and I'd tell her to get herself out and sure enough she would. Good thing she learned young, 'cause she's had to haul all the others out. I don't worry if Milly's with 'em."

"You don't go off and leave 'em alone in this shack . . . I mean, on this shantyboat, do you?"

"Sure," said Mrs. Foster. "Abe and I go peddling fish twice a week. That's the way we make a living. Milly stays here and takes care of the kids."

"How old is Milly?"

"She's twelve, goin' on thirteen," said Mrs. Foster.

"But she acts like she's twenty!" added Patsy.

"Patsy here is a real river rat!" Mrs. Foster went on. "She was born right in the middle of the Mississippi River. That was when we were at Nonconnah Creek, down below Memphis. That houseboat we had then was so small I called it the Cracker Box! All but two years of Patsy's life has been spent on the river. That girl never lived in town in her life until we went to River City, Illinois."

Mrs. Preston and her children looked at Patsy as if she were some kind of queer fish.

"How terrible!" said Mrs. Preston.

"One time she fell in and went under the barge and her daddy had to drag her out by the legs," said Mrs. Foster. "That time she spit enough water, you'd a thought she was a camel!"

The women laughed.

"I can dog paddle now," said Patsy. "Every day I go in the water and try it. I'm going to keep trying until I learn how to swim."

[34]

"Oh, you'll learn all right," said Mama. "All my kids are real fish when it comes to water. They've never been scared of the river."

"You folks want any milk?" asked Mrs. Preston. "With two cows, we got more'n we need. I got plenty to sell."

"Milk?" asked Mrs. Foster. "No, thanks, we don't need any. My kids don't like it. They haven't lived on land long enough to get to like it, I reckon." She took her visitor into the houseboat to look it over.

"Well, I never!" said Mrs. Preston, when they came out on the porch again. "You've got it better than I have. With bottled gas and everything!"

"It's our home," said Mrs. Foster. "I try to have it nice. Of course we don't hook up our electric lights unless we're stayin' a long time."

The sky began to cloud over, so Mrs. Preston took her children and hurried home, afraid of rain.

"I hope my clothes will get dry," said Mrs. Foster.

After the woman left, Patsy thought of the River City house and the neighbors there.

"I wonder how Pushcart Aggie's parakeets are," said Patsy. "I bet if I'd a asked her for it, she'd a given me one. A parakeet would make a nice pet for a houseboat."

"Yes, if the cat didn't eat it," said Mama.

"Remember the Millers and the time Janey found a pearl?" asked Patsy.

"It takes more than a pearl to make a mussel-fisherman rich," said Mama.

[35]

Patsy thought of the Cramer girls and Ginny and Lora and felt quite homesick. "When we goin' back to River City, Mama?" she asked.

"I don't know," said Mama. "Ask your daddy."

Just then the johnboat came round the end of the fish barge.

"Come on, Patsy!" called Milly. "You goin' with us?"

Patsy ran and jumped in the boat and Daddy started the outboard motor. They were headed down river to get shrimp for bait.

"It's fixin' to rain," called Mama. "Don't you think you'd better wait and go later?"

But her words were lost on the wind. The motor roared loudly and off they went. Soon they came to a sandy bank and got out. The two girls walked down the bank pulling the seine net. They scooped up the river shrimp and dumped them in the bait bucket. But Mama was right—it began to rain and the wind turned into a gale, so Daddy called them back to the johnboat.

"Storm coming!" he shouted. "Let's go home!"

The girls dropped everything and ran. *Chug-chug-chug* started the motor, then it slowed up and died. Daddy fussed with it, but it would not start again. He took the oars and began rowing. It began to pour. Daddy pulled and pulled, trying to get the johnboat around a fallen tree in the river, but every time the wind came, the waves jumped over the boat.

"Oh Daddy, we're gettin' soaked!" cried Patsy.

"A little rain won't hurt you!" Daddy laughed.

At last the boat got out in the river and Daddy kept on rowing. When they came to the chute, it was windy there, too. The wind had blown the clothesline down, and Mama was out picking the clothes up from the mud.

"Patsy!" she called. "You never propped the clothesline up the way I told you."

The girls helped pick the wet clothes up and made a dash for the houseboat. Bunny and Dan were hugging the porch posts to keep from being blown off.

"Shut the door! Shut the door!" cried Patsy, pushing everybody in.

"Oh, this wind!" cried Mama. "It's trying to blow all the furniture through the house and out the back door."

They all changed to dry clothes. Daddy moved the houseboat farther down the chute, out of the wind. Soon the storm was over. The wind and rain stopped as suddenly as it had begun

and the sun came out. So Daddy and Patsy went back to the same place. They found the bait bucket washed into the bank, full of mud and water, and the seine caught on a log. This time they got a good supply of shrimp.

Then Daddy saw some crows ahead on the sandy bank.

"They're after turtle eggs," he said, chasing them away. "Shoo! I can use those eggs myself." He found a circular hole on the bank, poked a stick in six or eight inches and uncovered twenty-four turtle eggs. They were round as marbles and had soft shells.

"Are they good to eat?" asked Patsy.

"Sure," said Daddy. "They're better to eat than the turtle meat. We're lucky to get these before the crows did."

Back at the houseboat, Daddy boiled the eggs and punched a hole in each to let the white run out like jelly. The yolk was cooked hard, but the white stayed liquid like milk. He baited hooks with the eggs, shells and all, as far as they went, then used shrimp. Baiting his hooks meant an hour and a half of work for Daddy. He sat on the edge of the fish barge and worked steadily and quietly. He had three trotlines, each in a square "line box." Each line had from eighty to one hundred short cords with hooks attached. He had to put bait on every hook. All the cords had to be carefully placed so they would not get tangled.

Tom, the cat, came sniffing up.

"Looky here!" said Daddy. "These shrimp are for the fish, not for you."

Patsy gave Tom a dish of shrimp all for himself. Then she fed her chickens and watered them. As soon as the hooks were baited, Daddy got ready to go out and set his lines. He put his knee boots on and took a can of gasoline to the johnboat. He put the line boxes in the boat. He dried the motor off and got it started.

"Hey, Patsy!" he called. "You goin' with me?"

Patsy came running and jumped in beside him. They chugged up river a half mile or so. Then Daddy turned the oars over to Patsy while he set his lines.

Patsy liked going out alone with Daddy. He treated her as if she were grown up. He didn't boss her the way Milly did. It was always quiet and peaceful out on the river alone with Daddy. He didn't talk much and neither did she, but they understood each other.

Each fish line had a heavy weight on one end to sink it in the water. Daddy threw out the other end, with a double-can buoy attached. The buoy floated on the waves and showed him the location of the line the next day. When the line was in place, all the short cords with the baited hooks hung down in the water to snag the fish.

On their way back, Daddy stopped by a log that was sticking out of the water. Patsy picked up three mud turtles and tossed them into the boat.

"More pets?" Daddy laughed.

"I can't ever get enough," said Patsy.

Early the next morning before breakfast, Patsy went out again to help Daddy run the lines and bring the fish in. He caught some big ones this time. One weighed eighteen pounds and one fifteen. He took them and those already in the fish box and packed them in the tub of ice in the trunk of the old car.

Mama was all dressed up in her good clothes, ready to go to town. Daddy hurried to change.

"Can't I go with you?" begged Patsy.

"No," said Mama, "you stay here. You kids are O. K. here."

"But Mama," said Patsy, "I want to go along. I want to help sell fish."

"We don't need you," said Mama.

"You goin' to leave us all alone here, Mama?" asked Patsy.

"You won't be alone," said Mama. "Milly will be here."

"Milly's so bossy," said Patsy. "She won't let me do a thing I want to. She won't let me go out in the johnboat or anything."

"Well, you can't swim," said Mama. "I'd worry myself to death if Milly wasn't here to pull you kids out."

"She can boss Dan and Bunny all she wants to," said Patsy. "They're just babies. I've got more sense than they've got."

"You listen to what Milly tells you," said Mama. "She knows how to cook and use the gas stove. You mind what she says and you won't get in any trouble."

"When will you be back?" asked Patsy.

"It'll be three o'clock if we don't stop for groceries," said Mama. "If we do, we won't be home till five. The fish markets are flooded now and won't buy fish. Daddy's got so many this time, we'll have to peddle them at people's houses till we sell them all."

Patsy looked sad as she watched the old Ford go up the river bank and away. The day would be endless until five o'clock. The houseboat was not like home with Mama away. She thought of her old Illinois friends, Ginny Cobb and the Cramer girls, and

[40]

the thought made her homesick. There were no children on Mayfield Creek except the Preston boy and girl who were not allowed to play by the river. Beyond the Preston house was a country store where a cranky old man named Stub Henderson sold groceries. But he had no family.

There was no one around but bossy Milly. Dan and Bunny had their toys on the back porch and played there all morning long.

Patsy took her turtles out of the fish box and lined them up on deck. She had twelve now. She pretended they were pupils in school and she was the teacher. Each time one moved out of his seat, she took her stick and made it go back. She tried to think up tricks, but the turtles did not respond. They were stupid, so she put them back in the fish box. She decided to catch skipjacks for bait.

Skipjacks were fish that barely hit the water. They flipped and jumped in a school of minnows, trying to catch them. Patsy got her pole and sat on the guard. The pole had a wire line with a grabhook—three hooks welded together. She began snagging the skipjacks. She had fourteen in her pail when Dan came out. In trying to go past her on the guard, he kicked the pail over.

"Now, look what you've done!" cried Patsy. "Spilled all my skipjacks!"

Dan ran round the guard and Patsy chased him. She caught him and ducked his head in a tub of wash water that was standing on the back porch. Then Dan took a dipper and began throwing water in her face. Patsy backed up and then, *splash!* Back she fell into the river!

Just what Mama said, she thought. *I'm always falling in.* She

[41]

bobbled about, trying to save herself. *If I could only swim! That's what Mama's been saying all along—I've got to learn how. But I don't know how to swim. That means I'm going to go down three times and drown.* She swallowed some water and began to choke. She thrashed her arms about wildly. *Where's Milly? Why doesn't Milly come? She's supposed to haul all the little kids out, Mama said. Mama won't worry if Milly stays home with us.* Patsy felt herself going down, but she didn't go down at all.

Somebody had hold of her arm. Somebody was pushing and shoving her. She reached up and got hold of the guard. A man's voice said, "I've got her." And she was lifted up on deck.

Now they turned her over and started pumping water out of

her. She wished they would stop. At last they did and she was able to rest and get her breath back. Then she opened her eyes.

There was Milly with frightened face, kneeling beside her. There was Stub Henderson, the cranky old storekeeper, staring down at her. And over on the leather couch, Bunny and Dan were holding each other and crying their eyes out.

"You're gonna learn to swim, young lady," said Stub. He sounded very cross. "I'm gonna learn you myself before this day is over."

When Patsy got up, she looked at Stub Henderson and said, "What you doin' here?"

"I was fishin' in my johnboat when I heard a big splash," Stub said. "I come over to get the biggest fish of all and it was YOU!"

Milly laughed, but Patsy did not think his joke was funny at all. She was worried about only one thing. "Promise me you won't tell Mama and Daddy," she begged.

Stub promised on condition that Patsy would learn how to swim.

"Come on, now," he said. "No time like the present."

"I'm tired," said Patsy. "I nearly got drowned just now."

But Stub would not listen to excuses. "Come on, I'll show you."

"I know how to dog paddle," said Patsy. "All Dan and Bunny can do is mud crawl." Reluctantly she put on her bathing suit.

"Dog paddling is not swimming," said Stub.

He meant business, so he anchored his boat out in the river, where the water was over Patsy's head. He showed her how to do the side stroke, and told her to swim out to him and he would catch her. Patsy was very scared, but she jumped in and tried it.

"Come on!" called Stub. "Keep comin'."

Patsy tried to make the strokes the way Stub told her, and was surprised when she reached Stub's boat. Stub moved it farther out, and she tried again. He gave her several pointers, and she tried to do it right.

"You're swimmin', kid! You're swimmin'!" shouted Stub.

Patsy swam back and forth several times. Dan and Bunny clapped their hands and even Milly was pleased.

"Now I won't have to pull you out any more," said Stub, as he paddled away in his boat. Patsy kept on practising after he left. Then she got tired, so she climbed up on the deck to rest.

"From now on," said Milly, "if you fall in, you can get yourself out."

When Mamma and Daddy got back at five o'clock, the children were excited over the news they had to tell.

"Patsy can swim! Patsy can swim!" they cried. They told how Stub Henderson came and gave her lessons. At first Mama would not believe it. Then she said, "It's about time you learned. Now I'll stop worryin' about you fallin' in. It'll be Little Abe's turn to learn next."

The very next Saturday, Patsy got her longed-for trip to town. Daddy slipped on the fish barge and sprained his ankle, so he decided not to go. Mama took Patsy with her.

It was a hot summer day. They drove through corn and tobacco fields. The tobacco was only a foot high and had not begun to sucker yet. The corn was getting tall and roasting ears were setting on. They passed orchards of fruit trees and soon came to Barlow, a small town. Main Street was lined with booths, and peddlers in cars. It was a busy place with people coming and going. Country people had brought vegetables, chickens, eggs, corn and other produce to sell. Town people came to buy.

Mrs. Foster and Patsy sat in the Ford and waited for customers. When one came, Mama got out and sold fish. Buying was brisk for a while, then it slackened.

"We'll have to go on to Kevil," said Mama, discouraged. "Daddy's better at selling than I am." Then she saw a familiar figure coming down the street. "There comes Mr. Cooper. He's been buying from us every week. Maybe he'll help us out."

Mr. Cooper owned the restaurant down at the corner.

"So this is the houseboat girl!" he exclaimed, patting Patsy on the back. "Got any fresh fish today, Mrs. Foster?"

He looked the fish over and said he would take all that were left in the tub. While Mrs. Foster was weighing up, a stray cat came along and sniffed at the fish. Patsy picked it up.

"Put that cat down, Patsy," said Mama. "Don't start messin' with a strange alley cat."

The restaurant man looked at Patsy again. "Is this the girl that likes pets so much?" he asked.

"It sure is," said Mama. "She just can't let 'em alone."

Mr. Cooper said, "You don't want a cat, girl. I'll give you a dog."

Patsy gasped. "You will?" she said. This was too good to be true. She dropped the cat hastily.

"Come with me," said Mr. Cooper.

Mrs. Foster laughed. "You're just fooling. We don't need a dog."

But Patsy was on her way to the restaurant. When she came back, she led a short-haired half-grown black dog on a rope. Mr. Cooper came back, too.

"We can't take a dog with us," said Mrs. Foster. "Our houseboat's crowded already."

Mr. Cooper laughed. "What's a houseboat without a dog?"

They all looked at the dog whose name was Blackie.

"Except for his white breast, he's the blackest dog I ever saw," said Mr. Cooper. "His hair is so shiny, it glitters. That dog's not scared of a thing—he's part hound and part just plain cur. Take him along with you, Patsy. I know you'll give him a good home."

Patsy could not find words to thank Mr. Cooper. When she and Mama got home, the children crowded round and patted Blackie on the head. Blackie wagged his tail, happy to have found good friends. Daddy said he looked like a mighty fine dog, but Mama kept on shaking her head.

"I've got enough kids without taking on a bunch of pets," she said.

CHAPTER IV

On the River Again

"We're goin' on the river again!" cried Dan.

"We are?" asked Patsy. She could hardly believe it.

There was brisk excitement in the air. Daddy was getting his motors tuned up and was putting things in order on the fish barge. Mama had done a good housecleaning in the houseboat and a big family washing on the river bank. While Daddy was baiting his lines for the last time, Mama got supper ready.

Only Milly did not want to go.

"We can't go yet," she said. "Our order hasn't come. I haven't a decent dress to wear to town."

Three weeks before, Mama and Milly had sent an order to a

mail order house for a dress for Milly and some sewing supplies. Every day Milly went to the Wickliffe post office, but no package had come.

"The postmaster said he would forward it," said Mama. "I told him we would stop at Columbus."

"That means we'll never get it," said Milly.

"I can't help it," said Mama. "Daddy's set to go."

Patsy shinnied up the "monkey pole" to the roof of the houseboat. Milly was already there, tying down fishing gear and nets. They saw Daddy go off round the bend of the chute.

"What's he setting his lines tonight for?" asked Patsy.

"To get a big haul of fish," said Milly.

"Are we taking smelly old fish with us?" asked Patsy. "Do we have to wait till Daddy runs his lines in the morning? I thought we were starting *early*."

"Daddy will bring them in by daylight," said Milly.

At supper Mama said, "We'll stop at Columbus, Kentucky, to sell our fish. That'll give us a little cash money to go on. Daddy's got a Kentucky fishing license, so we'll stop wherever we can in Kentucky and fish along the way."

"But if we're goin' somewhere, why can't we just hurry up and get there?" asked Patsy. "I just want to get to New Orleans *so bad!*"

"On the river nobody likes to hurry," said Daddy, who had just come in. "That's the good thing about it."

Patsy hardly took time to eat. She left the table and went out on the river bank to close up her chicken coop. It was dark now and the hens were inside. Dan helped her carry the coop to the cabin boat. Patsy called Blackie, the dog, and told him they were leaving next day. Blackie wagged his tail—it was all right with him.

That night everybody went to bed early. The next morning when Mama called the children to get up, Daddy was back with the fish, about thirty pounds. They ate breakfast by the light of the kerosene lamp. The houseboat was out in the river by the time the sun was up.

There was no one to wave to, no one to call good-bye. It made Patsy think of the time they had left River City. There was nothing permanent about river life. People on the river were always coming and going. *Here today and gone tomorrow,* as Daddy said. That big old river was always calling you to leave the river bank and go places. And nobody cared if you went or stayed. This time there were no close friends being left behind. Patsy could not mourn the loss of the Preston children who had never come to play by the river, and whom she knew only by sight.

Patsy sat on the front deck with Blackie and looked ahead. It was good to be on the river again. Life in Mayfield Creek had become dull and monotonous. On the river there was always something new to see. The river was full of bends. The houseboat was always turning corners and coming out on a new stretch. Every bend brought a new landscape, and often there were boats and barges to be seen. Patsy could not see much of the towns, they were too far back. Some were hidden behind the levees and she never knew they were there at all unless she looked at the map.

Sometimes she watched the buoys and navigation lights that marked the channel. The current in the Mississippi was unpredictable. The channel never seemed to follow the course of the stream itself. It wiggled around between the banks, often moving from one side to the other in a "crossing." In low water the crossings were well marked with buoys. Wherever the channel crossed the river, there was a river light or a day mark on the opposite bank. From each light or mark, the pilot set his course on the next one. One mark picked him up and called him, then sent him on to the next.

"There are so many lights and buoys on the river," said Daddy, "any fool can keep in the channel."

The lights were oil lamps, set on tripod posts twelve feet high, with a ladder to reach up. They burned round the clock with a flame so small it hardly showed by day, but was magnified by the globe at night. They burned kerosene and were tended every fourth day by a lamplighter.

In the middle of the morning, Patsy saw a ferryboat crossing the river ahead. She called Dan and told him.

"Is this a town we're coming to?" asked Dan.

Patsy looked at the map. Mama had taken map No. 3 out of the River Map book and tacked it up on the wall.

"It's Columbus, Kentucky!" cried Patsy. "We're there already. Boy! Don't I wish I could have a ride on that ferryboat!"

She and Dan and Bunny waved to the people on the ferry. Daddy nosed the houseboat in on the Missouri side below the ferry landing, and tied up under some willows. Mama had dinner ready and as soon as Daddy washed up, they ate. Across the river on the Kentucky side, they could see the high bluffs called the Iron Banks. Daddy said they were the highest bluffs between Cairo and Memphis. There was a muddy bar below them.

"Can we go to town? Can we go to town?" cried the children.

Mama and Daddy got ready to take the fish to Columbus. Mama said Patsy and Dan could go, so they quickly washed and put on their good clothes. Milly offered to stay on the houseboat and keep Bunny, if Mama would stop at the post office for the mail order package. Bunny cried when they left, so they promised to bring her candy.

They crossed the river in the johnboat and went to the fish market of Jim Tom Cheney, who bought all they had. Hearing a band playing, Mama and the children went off downtown, leaving Daddy at Jim Tom's. Several hours later they came back and found Daddy very impatient. "I want to set my lines tonight," he scolded.

"But Daddy!" cried Patsy. "Guess where we went!"

"They had a circus and we went to it," said Dan.

"A circus! What next?"

The children were so happy Daddy had to cheer up. All the way across the river they talked about the acrobats they had seen. When they reached the houseboat, they told Milly and Bunny about it. They gave Bunny the candy they had brought for her. Milly asked about the mail-order package, but Mama shook her head. There was nothing at the post office.

As soon as Patsy changed into her shorts, she started skinning the cat from the overhead porch beam.

"You'll be breakin' your neck now for sure!" said Mama.

The next morning Daddy got up early to run his lines. Before breakfast he had taken his fish catch over to Jim Tom Cheney. Now he had a little more change in his pocket. By the time the children had eaten their breakfast, the houseboat had resumed its voyage down river.

As Patsy dried the dishes, she looked out the window. It was like a moving picture, she thought, something different every minute as the banks started marching past. Each time she picked up a dish and looked out again, the scene had changed. The river made so many turns she was never sure whether she was looking at Kentucky or Missouri. Sometimes the sun shone in the windows over the sink and a little later it would be coming in through the windows opposite, as if it were afternoon. That was because the river was flowing north.

Milly got out the big fat mail-order catalogue and spent a long time looking at it. Mama had brought out her box of quilt patches and was cutting new ones.

"I hope my new dress comes soon," Milly said to Mama. "The dresses I get from the catalogue fit me better than those bought in the stores. The stores in these little old river towns are no good anyhow. My old dresses are all too small. I'll give them to Patsy."

"I don't want your hand-me-downs," said Patsy.

"Don't be too choosey, honey," said Mama. "Better be glad to get them."

"We've got to look on the map and see each town we're coming to, and go to the post office when we get there," said Milly.

[52]

"Did you order me a new dress, Mama?" asked Patsy.

"No," said Mama. "Shorts and T-shirts are good enough on the river. Nobody looks at river kids anyhow. You can wear Milly's old ones to town."

Milly happened to look up and see some pilings go past the window.

"Where's Daddy goin'?" she asked. "Is he fixin' to tie up?"

She ran out quickly.

Pile dikes were wide-spaced fences of heavy posts called "piling" driven out in the river. They were used by the U. S. Army Engineers to control the river's course. In some places they lined the banks like the teeth of a comb. They could be dangerous for a small boat pushed against them by a stiff current. But Daddy sometimes tied his big outfit to them for a short stop.

The water was slapping up against the hull. A lively current was passing on the chute side.

"What's Daddy going over to the pilings for?" asked Patsy.

"Daddy knows what he's doing," said Mama. "He's in the channel. He's going by the channel marks. He's lived on the river long enough to . . ."

But that time, Abe Foster made a mistake.

Suddenly there was a terrible jolt, followed by a long-drawn-out grating and grinding. The mail-order catalogue was knocked off the table and dishes were thrown out of cupboards. Mama nearly fell off her chair and Patsy landed *plunk* on the floor, with a broken plate in her hand. Bunny came staggering in with a bump on her head. Dan began to scream.

"A sand bar!" Milly shouted from the front porch. "We're on a sand bar!"

Nobody needed to tell Daddy or Mama either. Even the children knew it, down to little Bunny. They all went out to see. Daddy was furious.

"This crazy old river!" he scolded. "A sand bar in the middle, right in the channel! How can a fellow keep from hitting it?" He came up to the porch in his johnboat. "It's the cabin boat that's stuck, not the houseboat."

The mishap meant a long delay, but Daddy knew just what to do. He took the outboard johnboat and pulled the houseboat down to a towhead, leaving Patsy and the little ones alone on board. Then he brought Mama and Milly back to help him get the cabin boat off the sand.

"You'll have to wade out and push," Daddy said.

[54]

"Wade and push?" gasped Mama.

Much as she loved the river, Mama's love was purely an external one. She could not swim and she never ventured into the river if she could help it. To her, wading in the river was a terrible thing. Now, faced with the necessity of putting her feet in it, she was so scared she began to shake all over. But Milly had taken off her shoes and plunged in, so Mama had to do the same. First Daddy tried pushing with the oars, using main strength. But the sand was "crawly" and worked right out from under the paddle.

"Law me, I can see all the fish in the river!" Mama spoke in a low voice so Milly would not hear.

"Mama and I will push," Milly told Daddy. "When you start the motor to back it up, we'll both push."

Mama waded over. "But Daddy will run over us!" she cried.

"Don't be silly, Mama," said Milly. "He's going to *back*, I said."

The motor roared as Mama pushed and Milly pushed. But the boat, a heavy one twenty-seven feet long and ten feet wide, did not budge. After repeated trials it was still in the same place.

At the stern of the boat were two heavy barrels of gasoline. Daddy decided to move these to the bow. He also filled an empty fish tub with water. With this additional weight on the bow, he hoped to raise the stern and get the rudder off the sand. After this they tried again. He started the motor and with more pushing, the cabin boat finally slid back off the sand bar into deeper water.

"You wait here now, Mama," said Milly, "till I bring the johnboat."

Mama stood in the middle of the river with water all around her, petrified with fear. While she was waiting for the johnboat to come, she happened to look down. To her great surprise, she saw that the water was not even ankle deep! And when she returned to the houseboat, the bottom of her dress was not even wet.

Safely back in her cozy kitchen again, Mama laughed and laughed. "I thought I was drowned for sure," she said. "I could just feel all those fishes nibbling at my toes!"

Up spoke Dan. "I bet you wished Stub Henderson would come and pull you out the way he did Patsy!"

"Stub? Patsy?" cried Mama, surprised. "When did Stub pull Pasty out? Did Patsy fall in and nobody tell me?"

Milly and Patsy glared at Dan. Patsy grabbed his arm and

started to shake him. But the secret was out.

"Oh, gosh!" said Dan. "I wasn't supposed to tell. I forgot!"

"Oh well," said Patsy. "She's got to know some time."

So the whole story came out—Patsy's tumble in the creek, which led to her swimming lesson from old cranky Stub.

"Why didn't Stub tell me?" asked Mama.

"I made him promise not to," said Patsy.

"Well, since it's all over," said Mama, "I'm glad you can swim and won't have to be pulled out again."

Patsy put her arm around her mother's waist, looked up at her and said, "Want me to teach you how to swim, Mama?"

"NO!" cried Mama. "There are too many fish in the river!"

The children laughed.

The Fosters did not start on until the next day, and then they did not get far. The wind kept blowing the boat up river and was so strong that Daddy decided to lay over. He tied up in the chute nearby out of the wind because the boat was too hard to handle. That afternoon there was a storm. It rained hard and kept them all indoors.

After the storm, Milly and Patsy went exploring in the john-boat. They had not gone far before they saw a lamplighter's boat tied near a bank that had caved in. The tripod of the river light had fallen down and the lamplighter was hanging the lamp on a tree. When he came back to his boat, he called to the girls.

"You girls from the shantyboat over there?"

"Yes, we are," said Milly.

"Are you in trouble?" the man asked. "Can I tow you any-where?"

"We're O. K. now. You are a day late." Milly told him about getting stuck on the sand bar and he laughed.

"Where you folks goin'?" asked the lamplighter.

"Oh, just down river," said Milly. "We stop wherever Daddy takes a notion to stop."

"Real river people, eh?" asked the man.

"Sure!" said Milly. "My sister here was born in the middle of the Mississippi River."

"Oh Milly!" cried Patsy. "Don't tell everybody that."

The man laughed.

"Ever since the days of the flatboats, there have been all kinds of people goin' down river, huntin' adventure," said the lamp-lighter. "Nowadays some of them get more than they bargained for. Most every day I meet up with them and try to help 'em if I can. They come sailin' down in any old kind of craft—in a rubber canoe or a million dollar yacht or a big shantyboat outfit like yours. You're lucky if your Daddy knows what he's doin'."

"He's a real river man," said Milly with dignity.

"He's lived on the river all his life," added Patsy.

"O. K. then," said the lamplighter, waving his hand as he started off. "Have a good trip."

When the girls got back to the houseboat, they told Mama and Daddy about the lamplighter.

"That couldn't have been Seth Barker, could it?" asked Mama.

"No," said Daddy. "He's not as far north as this. His run is down along Arkansas."

"Wonder if we'll see Seth and Edie this trip," said Mama.

"I doubt it," said Daddy. "They never stay in one place very long."

"They're as bad as you, Abe," said Mama.

"Well," said Daddy, laughing. "The river keeps moving, why shouldn't I?"

Patsy studied the river map each day. Each new page was tacked to the wall and showed a new stretch of the river. All lights and buoys were clearly marked.

"If I could only teach Daddy to read . . ." said Patsy.

"What's the good of a map?" asked Daddy. "The channel has changed a dozen times since it's been printed."

"Well, it's fun to look at, anyhow," said Patsy.

"What's the next town we're coming to?" asked Bunny. Town meant candy to Bunny, so she could not get there too soon.

"Hickman, Kentucky," said Patsy. "I'll watch all the lights and tell you when we are getting near. 939—that's Williams light, and 937.3 is Samuel light. Hickman is right by Island No. 6."

The day wore slowly on. There were long stretches of revetments first on the Missouri, then on the Kentucky side. Revetments were banks paved with asphalt to prevent erosion, where the current raced swiftly by. They made progress difficult, because there was always danger that the houseboat might be smashed against them.

Sometime later, Patsy looked up from the mail-order catalogue and saw a light. "927.5—that's Henderson light. Why, we never stopped at Hickman at all! We're past it!"

"We're past Hickman?" cried Milly in dismay. She slumped in a chair and began to grumble. "I wanted to go to the post office for my package."

"It's too late now," said Mama. "Coming down river it's hard to get in and out of Hickman Bend, but we should have seen the town. It's a pretty place, high up on a hill, and there's a ferry, too. Looks like Daddy's aimin' to make New Madrid tonight."

"Why, that's way over on the next page," said Patsy, looking at the map book. "We'll go by a big island first, No. 8. That's still in Kentucky, but pretty soon we'll get to Tennessee." She turned the page.

Below Island No. 8, there were great sand bars for miles along the river and stretching inland, dotted with snags and fallen trees from previous floods. Tall grasses and willows grew on the higher parts. There were many birds—kingfishers, sea gulls, killdees and a few pelicans.

Mama came over to look at the map, and Patsy started explaining.

"When we get to the Kentucky-Tennessee line, there's a big loop in the river. New Madrid's up at the top in Missouri. The loop is in Kentucky."

"That's New Madrid Bend," said Mama. "Daddy says you can walk across that neck of land in thirty minutes, but it takes half a day to go around in a boat. The neck is only a mile wide, but it's nineteen miles around the loop, almost a circle."

"Too bad we can't carry the houseboat over," said Dan.

"Then we wouldn't get to stop at New Madrid," said Patsy.

Now they were traveling northeast, as if heading for Illinois again. It was a long hard pull to New Madrid and Mama thought they'd never make it. The wind was against them all the time, blowing them the other way, so it took twice as much gas to push the boat. Late in the day they came in sight of New Madrid and Daddy made the houseboat fast to some piling near the landing.

"I'm about out of food," said Mama. "I'll have to lay in a supply for two or three days. If we should get laid up in a storm, we'd have to eat."

"I'll have to fill up with gas, too," said Daddy.

"I want to go to the post office," said Milly.

"We want candy," said Dan and Bunny.

Patsy thought for a minute. "And I'd like a great big bunch of bananas," she said.

They all laughed.

CHAPTER V

Still on the River

"None of you can go," said Mama the next morning. The children began to wail, but it did no good.

"I'll get the ice and my groceries as quick as I can," said Mama, "and Daddy will ask the man at the fish market to call a gas truck."

"As soon as I fill up with gas," said Daddy, "we'll start down river. This is a bad place here, tied up to this piling."

"Can we go in swimming?" asked Patsy.

"No," said Daddy. "There's quicksand here—it's too dangerous."

"Oh heck!" said Patsy in disgust. "After I learn to swim, I

never get a chance to go in the water."

Off went Daddy and Mama in the johnboat to the town of New Madrid, pronounced New Mad'-rid. Patsy and Bunny were still in pajamas. They tumbled back into bed again. The houseboat always seemed empty with Mama gone.

"Anybody who wants any breakfast better come and get it," called Milly from the kitchen.

"I'm not hungry," said Patsy.

"Neither am I," said Bunny.

But they came out and ate just the same. Milly pulled Dan out of his cot and dragged him by one leg to the kitchen. Half asleep, Dan tried to eat, then ran back to bed. He took Tom, the cat, under the covers with him.

"You kids better get your clothes on," scolded Milly.

"Stop your bossing," said Patsy.

"Well, I'm boss when Mama's gone," said Milly.

"You're not gonna boss me any more," said Patsy. "From now on, I'm my own boss."

"Ha! Ha! That's what *you* think!" Milly laughed as she started to wash the breakfast dishes.

Patsy put on her clothes and went out on deck. She sat on the couch and put her arm around Blackie's neck. "Here comes a towboat!" she called. Bunny and Dan came running.

"A towboat!" Milly dropped the dishcloth and came out, too.

A big towboat was coming round the bend with a whole riverful of empty barges in front of it. It was going down river for a load of oil and going down very fast.

"Oh boy!" cried Milly. "We'll be knocked to pieces against

the piling. What can I do?"

Patsy and the little ones looked at Milly. She was boss after all, but her face was white and scared. Even Milly did not know what to do.

"Go away, you mean old towboat!" cried little Bunny, shaking her fist at it.

But the empties were coming closer and closer, and behind them came the huge clean white towboat, pushing hard. The captain up in the pilothouse gave a snort on the whistle as the tow came closer and closer.

"If he'll just hold to the outside of the channel . . ." said Milly under her breath, "maybe he won't tear us apart. . . ."

The children ran to Milly and clung to her as if she were Mama. Even Patsy was scared and looked to Milly.

"Can't you *do* something?" she cried.

But there was nothing at all to be done. Nothing but to watch fascinated as the huge towboat scraped past and the great waves came rushing toward the defenseless houseboat.

When they hit, the houseboat was thrown heavily against the piling. All four children were thrown off their feet and went sprawling. Dishes and pans fell inside and furniture was knocked over. The next minute the houseboat was pushed so far out that two ropes broke, the one from the stern to the piling, and the towline from the cabin boat to the houseboat. The third rope from the bow to the piling still held and the houseboat swung round and round.

Out on the cabin boat, the chicken coop was knocked down, the door had burst open and the chickens were thrown out. Some landed on top of the cabin and others fell into the river.

The children scrambled to their feet unhurt, just in time to see the towboat make the turning off Kentucky Point Bar. All they could see was her wash, and then she cut behind the bank and was gone. It had all happened so quickly, they were stunned. Blackie was barking, but Dan was the first to speak.

"You mean old captain!" he cried, shaking his fist. "We got just as much right on this old river as you have. Why couldn't you slow up? You just wanted to tear us to pieces!"

Then Patsy saw her chickens. "Oh look!" she cried. "My chickens! What can I do?" Before Milly could answer, Patsy saw the broken ropes. "Are we loose?" she cried, with fear in her eyes. "If we're loose, the current will take us down river without Mama and Daddy!"

Dan and Bunny began to wail.

"I'll try to find some rope," said Milly, "to tie us up again. She looked around. "But how can I get to the cabin boat?"

The second johnboat, the one without a motor, was out on the river floating away. There was no way to get to the cabin boat, so she was helpless. The houseboat was swinging round and round, and soon the frayed rope that held it, snapped in two.

"The rope's broken!" cried Patsy, clinging to Milly. "Now we're goin' down river for sure!" The little ones began to cry, and Blackie began to whine. Bunny ran inside and crept under the bed for safety. Dan crouched on the couch, his arms tight around the dog. The houseboat began to bounce around.

But Milly had no time to cry. She climbed up the "monkey pole" to look for rope on the catchall roof, but there was none there. Even if she found rope, she did not know how she could tie the houseboat up without a johnboat to take her to land. Up on the roof she found two long oars and brought them down.

"We'll try to keep it close in, if we can." She spoke quietly now to Patsy, handing her an oar. "We'll do what we can till Daddy gets here. Even if we float a ways, it won't hurt us any. Daddy can come after us."

Milly's judgment was good, so Patsy did not question it. She took the oar and tried to help. The houseboat bobbled about on the river, but had not gone very far, when the johnboat with Mama and Daddy in it appeared. Oh, how good it was to see them again! Before the sacks of groceries were unloaded, the story of the mishap had been told. Abe Foster was furious.

"If he'd a ripped us up or busted the hull open, he'd a had to

pay damages," Daddy said. "I've got as good a right here as the biggest towboat on the river. If there's anyone a shantyboater hates, it's one of them cocky towboat pilots!"

Daddy went straight to the cabin boat and soon the houseboat was tied up safe and sound again. Then he brought back the floating johnboat and was trying to rescue the chickens, when he heard a truck on the river bank honking its horn. He thrust four hens hastily into their coop. Then he shoved the boats, houseboat and all close to the bank to get gas. The man on the truck reached his long hose over to the barrels on the cabin boat and filled them.

The children kept talking about what had happened.

"Was I ever scared!" cried Bunny. "I ran and hid under the bed."

"Under the bed is a good safe place," said Mama.

"Look what's happened inside, Mama!" cried Patsy. "Everything is knocked to pieces."

They went in and began picking things up. Patsy threw the broken dishes into the river and watched them sink to the bottom.

"Mama," said Patsy thoughtfully, "I was glad Milly was here with us. She tried to do what she could."

"There was nothing she could do," said Mama.

"I listened to her," said Patsy. "I took the oar and paddled to keep us from going down river."

"I'm glad to hear that," said Mama.

"Do you know what, Mama?" Patsy went on. "Guess what I saw on that towboat! The cook came to the door of the galley and dumped out a bucket of potato peelings—to feed the fishes!"

Dan and Bunny laughed.

"And do you know what else I saw, hanging by the galley door?" said Patsy. "A great big stalk of bananas!"

"You saw all that?" Mama laughed.

"Oh Mama, those bananas looked *so good* . . ." said Patsy. "I just wanted me a banana *so -o- bad!*"

"I guess you weren't so scared, after all," said Mama. "I tried to buy bananas in town, but couldn't find any."

Bunny looked through the grocery sacks and found a sack of hard candy. The children filled their mouths until their cheeks puffed out.

"Did you go to the post office, Mama?" asked Milly.

"Yes," said Mama. "No package. I told him if it came to forward it to Tiptonville."

Soon Daddy had everything under control and the houseboat resumed its voyage. Patsy was brokenhearted to leave four of her chickens behind, but it could not be helped. She still had Shoo-Fly, Mrs. Cackle, Jenny Brown and Fluffy Tail. It was about ten in the morning when they started, but they did not go far. About two and a half miles south of New Madrid Daddy tied up. Nearby was a concrete bank with a sandy stretch at the bottom.

"What are we stopping here for?" asked Milly.

"I want to do the washing," said Mama.

The children did not wait to ask questions. They jumped off the deck and started running up and down the concrete. They shouted and sang while Blackie pranced and barked. They acted as if they had never been on land before.

The sun had come out but it was still windy—a good day to

dry clothes. Daddy hunted driftwood and built fires under the washpot and washtub. Then he stretched the clothesline from the back porch post to a tree. While Mama and Milly washed, the children chased Blackie up the river bank. They found some hedge apples on a bushy tree. The apples were green and hard like walnuts and the children wanted to eat them, but Mama made them throw them away. On the overhanging branch of an oak tree, Dan and Patsy practised skinning the cat and other acrobatic stunts. Soon the clothes were blowing merrily in the breeze, the line propped up with Mama's own precious clothes props brought all the way from Illinois.

Patsy stood by counting. "Five dresses, nine overalls, twelve shorts, nine shirts and four skirts . . ."

"And that's not all," added Mama, pointing to another pile.

Daddy caught some fish and Mama fried them over the campfire on the sand. Eating outdoors was like a picnic. The sun came out good and hot, so the children put on their bathing suits and waded and splashed in the water. Patsy swam out and came back many times. Mama gave the children soap for baths. She washed all their heads and they dried their hair in the sun.

About four o'clock, Daddy got ready to move on.

"We'll have to find a better harbor," he said. "We can't stay here. The wind would wash the houseboat up on this concrete and wreck it."

Farther on, a good harbor was found sheltered by high trees from the wind. It was rough that night and the family heard the waves slapping against the hull all night long. But aside from fallen branches of trees, no damage was done. The next day was stormy and rainy, so they stayed where they were. Mama did her ironing, Daddy worked on his engines while the children played. Dan and Patsy did acrobatic stunts until they were tired.

The next day Kentucky was left behind and Tennessee appeared on their left bank. It was still windy and the wind was up river as before. That made hard going, so progress was slow. The children were bored and restless because nothing happened. Then they heard a power boat coming.

"What the heck is that?" asked Patsy.

"It's a big cruiser," said Milly. "That's a Fleetcraft, isn't it, Daddy?"

"Looks like it," said Daddy. "Mighty pretty boat, and fast, too. Worth a lot of money. You got to be rich to have one of those boats, but I wouldn't trade it for my little old houseboat."

The big cruiser went sailing by, making the houseboat seem as out-of-date as a log-cabin flatboat of a century before.

"I'd like to have a ride on it just once," sighed Milly.

"Me, too," said Dan.

"You can have it," said Patsy. "Me and Daddy'll keep the houseboat. We don't want to go that fast."

Because of the wind, the day's run was short, only to Tiptonville, Tennessee. Daddy eased into the bank below the landing of the busy ferry. The town could not be seen as it was too far from the river. Daddy and Milly walked all the way to the post office to see if her package had come, but it wasn't there. Back at the houseboat Mama had started supper, when the children came running in to announce that Blackie was missing.

"Now, what next?" cried Mama.

"Blackie followed us up the hill," said Milly, "and I told him to go back. I didn't see him after that. Why don't you kids watch where he goes?"

"Oh, don't worry, he'll come back," said Mama. "Blackie knows the hand that feeds him."

Patsy could not wait for the dog to come back of himself. She ran up on the dock where there was a small store for boat supplies. The man there pointed up the hill.

"I saw a black dog go up that-a-way," he told her. "He was heading toward the ferry."

Patsy sent Dan back to the houseboat to tell Mama. When he returned, they hurried on. They came up to the landing barge, where a ferryboat was waiting. A line of six or eight cars began to move ahead slowly. The children looked around, but there was no sign of Blackie.

"Blackie! Blackie! Where are you?" cried Patsy.

"I bet somebody in one of those cars took him," said Dan.

"We'll look in their windows and see," said Patsy fiercely. "If we find him, we'll pull him out. They'd better not steal our Blackie." Tears filled her eyes.

They watched the cars going on the ferry, but there was no black dog in any of them.

"Maybe he went on the ferryboat," said Dan.

Patsy looked fearfully at Dan. "How will we get him off?"

"We'll go right on the boat and take him," said Dan, showing unexpected courage.

"But I'm afraid," said Patsy. "The ferryboat might go off with us."

"It'll go off with Blackie if we don't hurry," said Dan.

Patsy forgot her fears. The next minute she and Dan were running onto the ferryboat. The man who was putting the chain across the stern waited to let them on. He looked at them as if foot passengers were unusual.

"Where you kids going?" he asked gruffly.

Patsy stopped, her heart in her mouth. "We're not crossing over . . ." she began.

"Well, get off then!" the man scolded.

"But our dog . . . he's lost and we've got to find him," spoke up Dan, "and you can't stop us either!"

"Hey, what's this?" called a man passenger, laughing. "These kids holding up the ferryboat?"

"They're after a dog," said the ferry man. "Guess we'll have to wait."

Patsy and Dan had rushed to the front of the ferry, ducking around the crowded cars and peeking inside each one.

"Where is he? Oh, where is Blackie?" cried Patsy.

"Are you children looking for a black dog?" asked a strange lady. "There's one up front."

"Blackie, oh Blackie!" cried Patsy.

It took only a minute to find him. There was Blackie on the deck in front, looking off into space, quite unconcerned. He was all set for a voyage across the river. He turned his head when he heard his name called.

"Blackie!" cried Patsy. "What you doin' here?"

"Where do you think you're goin'?" asked Dan behind her.

Patsy picked the dog up and she and Dan rushed back. The

[72]

ferry man held the chain up until they dashed through.

"You found your dog, I see!" he said.

The man passenger laughed. "Now the kids are happy. They've got their pet back again."

Patsy and Dan watched the ferry pull away. Then Patsy looked down at the dog in her arms.

"Where were you going, Blackie?" she asked tenderly. "Were you going away and leave us?"

"He wasn't going away," said Dan. "He just got mixed up. He thought he was on the houseboat going down river."

"We'll have to watch him better after this," said Patsy.

There was great rejoicing in the Foster family when Blackie was brought back and the story told. They all laughed about Blackie wanting to take a ride on the ferryboat.

In the morning, they were off again.

Patsy thought now and then about her old home in a real house in River City, Illinois. The two short years of her life spent there now seemed like a dream. Even the memory of her best friends there was fading. She never talked about Ginny Cobb or the Cramer girls any more. She never mentioned Pushcart Aggie or Janey Miller, and her pearl. All that was buried deep in the short past of her childhood. The experiences of now and the present were so rich, she was not reminded of what had gone before.

Now her life was the river, the great Mississippi River which had claimed the souls of so many people before her, people of all kinds, all ages and stations. The river was a mighty force that challenged human beings and dared them to meet that challenge. All her life now was bound up in the river. Some days she just sat on the deck and dreamed.

In her mind was a confused jumble of impressions—willow trees and sand bars, wooded islands and towheads, snakes, turtles and fish, water birds in the shallows and land birds in the cottonwoods, pile dikes, asphalt banks and cave-ins, buoys and river lights and day marks. Once when they stopped she saw the bright eyes of a raccoon looking down from the branch of an overhanging tree, but Daddy would not let her get it for a pet.

It was hard to remember the days of the week, or what town they had been in or passed by. It was hard to remember where particular events had taken place. One day passed and another came. The Foster family kept going without seeming intent or purpose, just to keep going. Sometimes Patsy wondered if they would ever stop and if she would ever live in a house again.

Now she saw the people on the river banks with a fresh eye. She would see children stopping their play and staring as the houseboat went by. She would see a mother hanging the wash out on a line, but the line was tied to a little house with roses blooming over the doorway and not to a houseboat. She would see the cars moving along the road with people riding in them, and now and then a train with people looking out the windows.

She felt sorry·for the land people now. They did not know what they were missing when they stayed in one place all the time. She pitied the children because they had only a yard or a few streets to play in, instead of a great river that went on and on even to the ocean. She knew they had stores and movies to go to, and some had television in their homes, but all that was stupid and dull beside the richness of outdoor life. Didn't they wish they

could be on a boat like her, to stand on the deck and fish, to jump off the deck and have a swim? Didn't they know how exciting it was to live on a houseboat?

One day she said to Daddy, "Don't you feel sorry for those people over there?"

"Why?" asked Daddy.

"Because they can't go on the river like us."

Daddy patted her shoulder. "Spoken like a real houseboat girl," he said. "Once you feel sorry for the people on the bank, that means the river has got you for good."

But even though the river had taken hold of her, as Daddy said, there still remained one thought buried under all her river experiences, a thought that teased and tormented her, and would give her no peace. It was the thought of a house, a permanent home on land. What if, after all, the people on the bank were right?

There were long hours when nothing happened at all. The houseboat drifted along steadily and Daddy often sat lazily on deck. The children ate meals when Mama called. They were always wanting a town and it seemed a long ways there. They quarreled over little things—which chair or bench to sit on, who should wash or dry the dishes. Patsy did not look at the river map or notice the numbers on the river lights any more. She watched the water birds in the shallows and the flocks of red-winged blackbirds in the trees. If she waited long enough, there would be a town.

The last one in Missouri was Caruthersville.

Caruthersville meant town, and town meant getting ice and

groceries and meat, but Caruthersville held an unexpected surprise. On the way back to the river, they stopped at a fish market.
Daddy had no fish to sell, because he had no Missouri fishing
license, but he wanted to talk to the other fishermen there. The
fish market was run by a woman who said her name was Aunty
Ruth. She invited the children to her house nearby and let them
watch television. While they watched, she gave them cold drinks.

"You like livin' on the river?" she asked.

"Oh yes," said Patsy.

Then they thanked her and followed Daddy back to the
houseboat.

CHAPTER VI

Down, Down, Down the River

"When are we going to stop and stay a while?" asked Patsy. "I'm tired of bein' in the boat all day long."

It was Mama who answered. "Oh, we'll look for a nice place under the river bank somewhere along."

"In a town?" asked Patsy. "Will we get a house again?" Sometimes her longing was so great, she just had to talk about it.

"I've got a place in mind," said Daddy. He turned to Mama. "Remember that chute down by Luxora where we used to stop sometimes?"

"O'Donald Bend," said Mama, "near Ashport Ferry. At Ashport on the Tennessee side is where we met Seth Barker and his wife."

"Yes," said Daddy. "When our engine broke down, I went over to Ashport and tried to get help. I met Seth and he told me where to get my dry shaft welded."

Mama went on, "Seth said to me, 'Come on up to the house.' I didn't want to go but I did. When you came for me, I didn't want to leave, I liked Edie so much. We was like old friends the minute we set eyes on each other. That was ten years ago when Milly was about two. She was so fat, she was a load to carry."

"We never went in the chute that time," said Daddy.

"No," said Mama, "that was another time, when Dan was little. We stopped in the chute to get some stuff, and the water was up to the willows. We saw people there and hogs, chickens and dogs and we kinda liked it. We was goin' up river in January and we stayed all night at the end of the chute. Next day we tried to find the Barkers. An old man told us where to find them. It was hard work shovin' willows up to their door, but we made it. Seth had the job of lamplighter by that time."

"Then two years ago, they'd moved back over to Tennessee again," said Daddy. "Seth Barker was never a man to stay in one place for long."

"It would do my heart good to see Edie again," said Mama. "Let's stop at O'Donald Bend and hunt them up."

"Like findin' a needle in a haystack," said Daddy, "but we'll take a look at that chute."

"And maybe stop and stay a while?" asked Patsy eagerly.

Daddy patted her on the back. "We just might do that, honey."

The houseboat made good headway down river, around Island No. 18, and came to Cottonwood Point ferry in lower Missouri, where Daddy had to stop for some minor repairs. The children begged Mama to let them go to the store at the ferry landing.

"What for?" asked Mama.

"We want to see what's up there," said Patsy. "See the town and the stores and the houses and the people."

"There's no town at all," said Mama, "nothing but a country road leading to the ferry."

"Daddy said there's a gas station and a store," said Patsy.

"Gimme a nickel, Mama!" begged Dan and Bunny.

"Gimme a nickel, too," begged Patsy, bringing Mama's purse.

"Hush! All I got is pennies," said Mama, giving some to each. "Go spend them if that's any fun."

Bunny dropped one of hers. "Where's my penny?" she cried. Patsy picked it up.

Mama said, "Patsy, give it to Bunny."

Patsy who was running, threw the penny behind her. Bunny finally found it, said it was not hers and began wailing for the other one. Mama watched them as they ran, followed by the dog and cat.

"Don't let Blackie get lost," she called after them.

In half an hour they came back with bubble gum and began smacking it. Suddenly Dan burst out, "I know what bubble gum's made out of!"

"What?" asked Patsy.

"Dead horses!" said Dan.

"Oh!" cried Patsy. "How horrible!" She spat hers into the river. "Next time I'll buy gumdrops."

Patsy went out to the back porch where Mama was peeling

potatoes. She sat down quietly beside her and started to talk.

"There was a girl up there at the store, Mama," Patsy said, "and I didn't like her at all."

"Why not?" asked Mama. "Anything wrong with her?"

"She had a pretty dress on," said Patsy, "and a gold ring on her finger."

"Well, what of it?" asked Mama. "Anything wrong with that?"

"No, but . . ." Patsy began. "She wasn't nice. She called us *river rats* 'cause we live on a houseboat." Patsy began to cry and Mama took her in her arms to comfort her.

"There's just as good people on the river as on land," said

Mama, "and don't you ever forget it, honey."

Soon the houseboat was on its way again. Arkansas was now on the west bank, although in some places, due to a changed course of the river, Tennessee was on both banks. Around Island No. 21 and on through Needham Cut-off the current was swift. The swiftest current of the whole river was between Caruthersville and Memphis. There were so many bends in the river now, the course of the houseboat was constantly changing direction.

The river was never without drama, and often it came unexpectedly.

"Look at the fishermen," cried Dan, as they rounded Barfield Bend.

"That's jug-fishing," said Milly. "See their jugs floating?"

Several men were out, each in his own johnboat. Gallon jugs of glass, with stoppers in them and baited lines attached to the handles, had been tossed overboard. The fishermen floated slowly along, dumping out one jug after another about twenty feet apart. They had piles of jugs in their boats, each with its baited line wrapped around it. The men were kept busy following the jugs as they bobbed about in the river.

Daddy sat on deck, letting the houseboat drift slowly by on the current. Suddenly a sound like the firing of a shotgun was heard.

"He's got one—a big fellow!" cried Patsy, excitedly. "Look! It's pulled the jug under!"

A catfish under water had got hold of the bait. When the jug was jerked under, the water came together behind it with a loud crack. The jug stayed down as the fish ran with it and came up

[82]

farther on. Then it went down again. The fish was putting up a hard fight. The man kept following it in his boat, but was waiting for the fish to wear itself out. Finally the fish gave up, came to the top of the water and floated on its back. The man pulled it in and held it up.

"Look at that!" cried Daddy. "That's a thirty pounder, I bet. Only the biggest ones can pull those jugs under."

It was late when Daddy tied up and came in to dinner. He heard the sound of a motor and looked out the back door.

"Look at that big cruiser coming," he said. "It's throwing waves as high as the trees!"

The powerful boat came up and passed swiftly by.

"That's that same Fleetcraft we saw up near Tiptonville," said Milly. "I'd know it anywhere. They were so much faster than us, they left us far behind. What's held them up, I wonder?"

"Engine trouble, probably," said Daddy. "Those fancy new boats are not all they're cracked up to be. Those people have probably been held up waitin' for a mechanic to take their engine apart and put it together again. They're probably headin' for Florida by way of the Gulf of Mexico. Hope they don't get drowned before they get there."

After the cruiser passed, everything was quiet again. The river was wide like a great lake, and the banks were so far away, they were just a line of green. It was hot, so Patsy sat down on the guard and swung her feet in the water to cool them.

"Take your feet out of that water," called Mama inside.

Patsy obeyed. "Mama can see clear through the walls of the houseboat," she told Dan.

[83]

After a while, Mama came out on the porch, where Daddy was sitting.

Suddenly Patsy felt homesick. If she could only see River City again! She sat down by Mama who was busy with her mending.

"Mama," said Patsy, "remember our house in River City?"

"Yes," said Mama, "I was glad to see the last of it."

"Remember those flowers I planted in that rubber tire in our yard? Pushcart Aggie gave me the seed."

"Yes," said Mama, "zinnias and they was real purty, too. But they died because you didn't water 'em, it was so hot last summer. I coulda fried an egg on our front steps any time."

"River City's in a low hole," said Daddy. "It never gets a breath of air all summer long. That house was as hot as a furnace. If there's anything I hate, it's bein' cooped up in a house!"

"But don't you *like* a house, Daddy?" asked Patsy. "With a yard and flower beds and trees around it?"

Daddy turned to look at the girl. "We've had two houses up there in Illinois and I wouldn't give you a fish barge for either one of 'em. Why are you so crazy about a house, girl? You liked it on the river all along . . . I thought I brought you up to be a houseboat girl!"

"But in town," said Patsy, "there's something for children to do. You can plant seeds and watch 'em grow. You got friends to play with, there's movies to go to . . ."

"Yes," said Daddy, "in town my kids are on the go, and I don't know where they go or what they're doin'. In town they might do mean things—break in stores or steal things."

"I wouldn't," said Patsy. "Milly wouldn't, and Dan and Bunny

[84]

wouldn't. We're all pretty good, Daddy."

"My kids are not angels," said Daddy. "They'd go where anybody goes, especially Dan. He's worse 'n a puppydog."

"When we've got you on the houseboat," said Mama, "we know where you're at."

"There's nothin' like the river," Daddy went on. "I've tried other things. I worked in timber, I had a hog business, I did farming with a tractor, I worked in a factory in Detroit, Michigan, but I couldn't stick it. I'm a born fisherman. If I was down and out, I'd bum fifty cents off somebody and buy me a trotline and start fishin' all over again!"

Patsy laughed. "I like fishin' too, but still—a house is nice."

"We made the mistake of stayin' in that house in River City for two years," said Daddy, looking at Mama. "That's the longest I ever lived on land since I was eighteen years old. Two years in a house—that's what has spoiled this girl. And here I thought she was a real river pal of mine."

"I still am." Patsy put her arm around his neck and hugged him. "It'll be nice to get back again, won't it?"

Daddy looked at her, startled.

"Back again? Where?" he asked. "To River City? Why, we just come away."

"I like bein' on the river for the summer," said Patsy. "It's a nice vacation. I told Ginny Cobb and the Cramer girls we'd be back by the time school starts."

Daddy said again stubbornly, "We just come away. We won't talk about going back yet."

There the subject ended.

It was below the Barfield revetment, where the channel crossed the river to the Tennessee side that Daddy spotted a sturdy boat with a closed cabin tied up to a tree near Wardlow Pocket Navigation Light. A man was coming down the bank to get into the boat. He stopped and looked when he saw the houseboat outfit coming down river. As it came closer, he raised his arm and waved.

"It's Seth Barker!" Daddy shouted. "It's Seth Barker or I'll eat my boots! He's out tendin' his lights!"

It was too good to be true. Daddy pulled in at the bank and soon the two men were shaking hands.

"If it ain't old Abe Foster!" cried the lamplighter. "You're a sight for sore eyes." He came on board to see Mama and the children. It was a happy reunion meeting an old friend.

"I was keepin' my eye open for you," said Abe Foster. "I figgered I might see you if you still had this run. Where you livin' now, in Arkansas or Tennessee?"

"We're at Ashport Ferry Landing in Arkansas," said Barker. "Got a houseboat now, but beached it up on that hill. I've got a forty-five-mile round trip to make—sixteen lights, fourteen kerosene and two battery lights. I go south to Cook's Island, that's No. 30, off Osceola, and up this way to about three miles above Tomato. Where you folks headin' for this trip—Memphis, New Orleans, Mexico, the West Indies or South America?"

"Not so far," said Foster. "Not even to Louisiana. I can't understand all that French they speak there."

"I'd sure like to see Edie again," said Mama, "and show her how the children have grown."

[86]

Seth Barker pulled Patsy's hair. "Just like weeds," he said. He patted Dan on the back. "Little Abe is sure gettin' big."

"We're headin' for O'Donald Bend tonight," said Foster. "Can we make it before dark?"

"Better get a move on," said Barker. "I'll tell Edie so you two women can get together." He chugged off in his power boat.

It was getting dark when the houseboat passed the little town of Tomato, high up on the bank. A few lights could be seen in the windows of houses. The Arkansas banks were high here, with several cave-ins. In one place a sinker barge was tied up to a heavy post. The barge's derrick lifted concrete slabs from the deck of a second boat and sank them into the bank for reinforcement. The men were working all night under a bright spotlight.

At the Bend of Island No. 25, darkness fell.

"There comes a big tow behind us!" cried Milly.

Mama and the children looked up river and saw it coming around a point about a mile back.

"That's not a tow," said Mama, as it came closer. "It's all lighted up. Looks like an excursion boat to me."

"It's lightin' up the whole sky!" cried Patsy, clapping her hands.

There were no barges ahead, and soon the great boat loomed up white and startling in the dusk of evening. Daddy saw it coming and, anxious to escape its wash, pulled over toward the bank. When the big boat came close, the children could read the name on the side.

"It's the *Delta Queen!*" cried Patsy. "The *Delta Queen!*"

"She comes from Cincinnati and she's bound for New Or-

leans," said Mama. "I've seen her lots of times. She's one of the last two-packet boats on the Mississippi and the Ohio. Wonder what she's doin' down here now. She makes most of her trips in the wintertime, takin' people to Mardi Gras in New Orleans."

All the children stared. The *Delta Queen* had four decks and there were bright lights in all the windows. Music was playing and they could see women in bright-colored evening gowns dancing with men in black coats. It was a beautiful and thrilling sight.

The children waved and called out, and wondered if the people could hear them. A man threw something overboard, but it fell in the river and was gone. And then the boat was almost past and the great big paddlewheel at the stern was splashing all wet and shiny in a whirl of spray. All too soon the beautiful vision was gone, faded away like a dream. It was gone away down river, leaving only a great wash behind. The houseboat bounced up and down on the waves, then righted itself with no damage done.

"*That's* the way to go to New Orleans," said Patsy emphatically. "When I get big, I'll go to Cincinnati and take a ride on the *Delta Queen.* That's the best boat on the river, the queen of them all."

The houseboat looked crude and shabby after the excursion boat had passed. The children were tired but would not go to bed. Milly and Mama hung lanterns out when it grew dark— a green light on the right of the fish barge and a red light on the left of the houseboat. Daddy put a white or open light on the tail of the outfit.

"If something happens and you have no light," said Mama, "you don't have no show."

"Will we get there soon?" asked Patsy, sleepily. "I want to see the place we're gonna stay a while. I want to put my chickens out on the bank. And Blackie, too—we're all tired of this old houseboat."

"It won't be long now," said Mama. "Once Daddy finds that chute called Canadian Reach, we'll soon be at O'Donald Bend."

The children were sound asleep when the houseboat slipped into the cove and the motor was stilled. Only the quiet lapping of the waves around the hull and the sleepy chirping of a bird in the willows broke the silence.

[89]

CHAPTER VII

O'Donald Bend

The next morning Patsy heard the cat meowing at the house-boat window. Daddy let him in and he came over to Patsy's bed and got in with her. Patsy dozed off again. Then the oven door in the kitchen banged. Daddy must be taking biscuits out of the oven. Tom the cat heard it, too, and ran out to eat breakfast with Daddy. He lifted his paw and said *meow.* Daddy said, "I can't hear you." Tom scratched his claws on Daddy's pants leg and Daddy fed him pieces of bacon.

Patsy dressed and went out. She was the first one of the children up.

"How you like it here, honey?" asked Daddy. He got up to

go to the fish barge. "Pretty nice, eh? You like it?"

"I don't know yet," said Patsy sleepily. She picked up a biscuit and a piece of bacon and followed him out on the porch. She took a look around and soon came in again.

"Where's our house?" she asked Mama. "There's none here."

"We don't need a house," said Mama. "We've got the biggest houseboat on the river."

"There's no town here," said Patsy.

"There's a country store," said Mama, "and lots of cotton farmers livin' up the river road. The school bus goes along here and picks up all the kids and takes them into Luxora to school. Luxora's a right nice little town about eight miles away."

Patsy had not thought about school for a long time. Now she remembered Miss Norton in River City. She thought of her birthday party when she had turned nine. Mama had sent a note to Miss Norton and she said yes, she could have one. Mama took a nice cake, boxes of ice cream, muffins and trinkets from the dime store. The children in Patsy's class played games and had a good time. Patsy got many presents. All that seemed a long time ago.

"When does school start?" she asked suddenly.

"The last week of August, probably," said Mama.

"Well, we can't stay here very long then," said Patsy. "We'll just have to turn around and start right back up that old river again."

"We're not going back to Illinois," said Mama quietly.

"Why not?" asked Patsy.

"It's too hard to push a big houseboat up river," said Mama.

"But we got to go back!" cried Patsy. "We *live* there. We've got our house there. I go to school there and I like my teacher."

Mama decided she might as well let Patsy know.

"We *sold* the house," she said. "We had to sell it to pay Daddy's debts."

Patsy's heart sank. "It's not ours any more?"

"No," said Mama cheerfully. "So we can't go back. That shelling up there was too hard on Daddy's back. He wanted a change."

"How will he make money?" asked Patsy.

"Selling fish," said Mama.

"Selling fish?" said Patsy. "Smelly old things . . ."

"There ought to be good sale for fish in a place like this," said Mama. "All the cotton pickers will come and buy."

Dan and Bunny were outside wading and splashing in the water at the river's edge. Milly was helping Daddy get his fishing gear out. Patsy came out on the porch and slumped down on the leather couch.

Below a bank of cottonwoods and willows, the houseboat was securely tied. The chute at O'Donald's Bend was as wide as a small river. Island No. 27, also called Fork-a-Deer Island, on the other side, was densely wooded. Birds were singing in the trees. The sun came out bright and hot.

"Well, here we are, honey!" Daddy called to Patsy from the fish barge. "How you like this place? Want to stay here a while, little river rat?"

To be called a *river rat* always gave Patsy a little stab of pain. But when Daddy said it lovingly, it was different. He was not

[92]

teasing her or calling names. He was loving her and using her pet name. But this time she sulked and did not answer.

"What's the matter, honey? Cat got your tongue?"

Still Patsy did not answer.

"I thought you was a river pal of mine," said Daddy. "Gonna help me set my trotlines this evenin'?"

"No, I'm NOT!" cried Patsy. She got up and flounced indoors, banging the screen door behind her.

Daddy looked after her, scratching his head. "Now, what's eatin' her, I wonder?"

He came in and passed by her where she lay on her bed, with her face turned to the wall. He changed his clothes and went up the river bank to catch a ride to town. He wanted to get his Arkansas fishing license the first thing.

Mama called from the kitchen, "Go take care of your chickens, Patsy. Move the coop up on the bank. If there are any eggs, bring them in."

Patsy got up. "But if we're not stayin' here . . ." she began.

"We *are* stayin' here," said Mama, "for a while anyway, to see if the fishing's any good. So make up your mind to that."

Reluctantly Patsy went out and called Dan. They took the chicken coop up on the bank and set it on an old sawed-off stump. Patsy opened the door and turned the hens out.

"They'll all run off in the woods and you'll never see them again," somebody said.

Patsy looked around and saw a strange girl staring at her. She was about ten, tall and thin and pale, and she had a mass of tangled blond hair. Patsy stared back and did not speak. She

[93]

sent Dan to get a hammer and some nails. When he returned, she nailed two nest boxes onto a tree near the coop. She pulled long grass and filled the nests.

"They'll lay all over the woods," said the strange girl. "They'll never go in them boxes."

"What do *you* know about it?" asked Patsy.

"You'll never see your chickens again," insisted the girl. "People will steal 'em, snakes and weasels and possums will eat 'em."

"Look!" said Patsy, pointing to the hens. "Are they runnin' off?"

The four hens stood watching, as if ready to lay their eggs.

"They been moved around so much, that's all they know—their nests," said Patsy. "Want to know what their names are?"

The girl's mouth opened in astonishment. "They got names?"

"This one's Shoo-Fly, and that one is Mrs. Cackle," said Patsy. "And there's Jenny Brown and here's Fluffy Tail."

The girl could not think of a thing to say. Two of the hens jumped into the nests.

"The varmints will get all their eggs," said the girl.

Patsy did not argue. She told Dan to go get a rope. She acted as if the strange girl were not there at all. Dan shinnied up the tree and tied the two ends of the rope to a horizontal branch. It made a nice rope swing. Patsy sat in it and swung back and forth. Then she picked up a chicken, tucked its head under its wing and perched it on the rope swing.

"I got to go pack Mama some wood in," she told the chicken. "You stay right here till I get back. Come on, Dan, let's get lots of wood. Mama wants to do a big washing."

They hurried away and began to pick up dead branches of trees. Dan brought a hatchet and they chopped them. They made a pile halfway up the river bank. All this time the strange girl stood watching them.

"I wish she'd go away," Patsy said to Dan.

"I don't like her," said Dan. "Do you?"

"No," said Patsy. "She thinks she knows it all."

They went over to the rope swing. The hen was still perched on the rope, its head still under its wing, the way she had left it. Patsy lifted the hen and put it in one of the nests.

"Jeepers!" exclaimed the girl. "How do you do that?"

Patsy tossed her head. "It's all in knowin' how!" She and Dan went back to the houseboat.

After a while the girl went away. But when Mama sent the

children to the store to buy some groceries, they saw her again in the road. This time there were other children with her, an older boy in ragged overalls and two little girls with very dirty faces. They stared at the newcomers.

Patsy turned to Dan. "I don't like this place, do you?" she asked.

"No," said Dan, "I just hate it. I hope we'll go down river tomorrow."

When they came out of the store with their bags of groceries, Patsy dropped one. The strange girl ran and picked it up. It had bananas in it.

"I'll tote it for you," the girl said in an eager voice.

She followed them down the river bank, leaving her brother and little sisters behind. She stopped at the stage plank, uncertain what to do. Patsy and Dan walked round the guard to put their groceries in the kitchen, then they came back. The girl handed Patsy the bag of bananas.

"My name's Joella Harris," she said, trying to be friendly. "What's yours?"

"Patsy Foster," said Patsy, "and he's Dan Foster."

"You *live* here?" asked the girl.

"Sure, why not?" said Patsy, on the defensive. She turned quickly and went inside.

Mama, who had been listening by the door, said, "Give that girl a banana."

"Oh, Mama, not a *banana!*" cried Patsy. "I don't even *know* her!"

"She helped you bring the groceries, didn't she?" said Mama.

[96]

"Yes . . . but . . ."

"Give her a banana," said Mama sternly.

Patsy went out and crossed the stage plank, where the girl was waiting. Grudgingly she held out a banana, a precious banana that she herself liked so much. "Here!" she said.

The girl turned away and refused to take it.

"All right, then!" snapped Patsy. "If you don't want it, I'll . . ." Quickly she stripped the banana and began to gobble it down in large bites.

"I can have all the bananas I want," said the girl. "I don't want any of yours."

"O. K. then," said Patsy.

But Joella did not go away. She still stood there.

"Where you folks goin', anyhow?" she asked, filled with curiosity.

"Down the river just any place we feel like," said Patsy. "We don't have to stay in one place the way you do. Our house floats. It doesn't set on posts in the ground like the houses round here."

"It looks *almost* like a house," said Joella.

Patsy frowned. "I wish it was a house," she said.

"You don't like livin' in a houseboat?" asked Joella.

"Oh sure," said Patsy. "Course I like it. I got to."

"But you'd rather live in a real house," said Joella.

"No, sir!" cried Patsy, fiercely. "Most people are not half as lucky as we are. They can't take their houses with them when they go places. We're regular *snails!* We take our house right along wherever we go." She looked at the strange girl and began to brag a little. "*You* got to stay in one place all the time. I feel sorry for *you. You* can't keep goin' the way we do. Why, we can even go all the ways to New Orleans if we want to."

"Where's that?" asked Joella.

"Why, don't you know?" asked Patsy. "Don't you study geography? I can find it on our river maps. It's in Louisiana, just above where the Mississippi flows into the Gulf of Mexico."

"Oh," said Joella. "You goin' there?"

"No," said Patsy. "We're stayin' here . . . I think."

"I'm glad," said Joella softly.

After Mrs. Foster put the houseboat in order, she decided to hunt up her old friend, Edie Barker, the lamplighter's wife. Milly went along as far as the store, found some girls her own age there and went off with them to one of their houses. Mrs. Foster asked the man at the store where to find the Barkers. He pointed up the dirt road toward Ashport Ferry Landing.

"They got a houseboat settin' right next to a cotton field," the man said. "You can't miss it."

Mrs. Foster and Patsy started up the road, with Dan and Bunny coming behind. A car caught up with them, passing in a whirl of dust to go to the ferry. The cotton beside the road was in bloom now. Patsy picked a blossom and put it in her hair. Passing several tumbledown farm buildings, they soon saw a houseboat on the left ahead. It was perched high on the bank, resting on heavy posts. Patsy did not need to be told why the houses in Illinois and Kentucky and Arkansas along the Ohio and Mississippi Rivers always stood on posts. That was because of high water every year.

There stood Mrs. Barker on the little back porch with a broom in her hand.

"Well, if it's not Liz Foster!" she cried. "Seth told me he seen you folks comin' down river and said you'd hunt us up."

The next minute they were all inside, and the two women were in each other's arms, and the children were trying to remember Aunt Edie. The Barkers' houseboat was much smaller than the Fosters'. It had three rooms, kitchen, bedroom and living room. It was tiny and cozy, and held a lot of furniture, including a TV set and a sewing machine. Aunt Edie was a plump good-natured woman of fifty, with hair already turning gray.

"We're always stoppin' along the river, huntin' folks up," said Mrs. Foster. "Usually we find 'em, but sometimes it's a hard job. We were afraid you folks had gone off again by this time."

"Law me!" exclaimed Mrs. Barker. "We been all over the map the last few years. We used to be at Ashport and got sick of it, so we went to Fort Pillow. Then we came back and lived in a tent at the head of this chute—you found us there, remember? Then we went to Louisiana for about a year. That state's plumb full of houseboats, but it's so wet, it gives you rheumatism."

"Seth is like Abe," said Mrs. Foster. "He's as crazy as Abe is— been all over and come back again like us."

"Seems like Seth is never satisfied," said Mrs. Barker. "In the woods it was too lonesome. Seth likes to talk and there was no one but me. Then he tried Louisiana 'cause he was born and raised there . . ."

"How long you been here?" asked Mrs. Foster.

"About eight months," said Mrs. Barker. "We just got this houseboat last winter. Seth paid five hundred dollars for it."

"It's nice and cozy," said Mrs. Foster, "for just you two.

[100]

Wouldn't be big enough for a family of kids like mine."

Mrs. Barker asked the children how old they were and passed around cookies. Then they went out to play and the two women talked alone.

"How you makin' out, really, Edie?"

"Purty good," said Mrs. Barker. "Seth gets a hundred and eighty-six dollars a month as lamplighter, but he has to furnish his own boats and motors and his own gas and oil. That doesn't leave too much for us. So I figgered if we stayed here in Arkansas this fall, I could help out by pickin' cotton in my spare time. One woman told me she makes sixty dollars a month at it. Of course I'm gettin' old and can't pick very fast, but . . ."

"I just won't pick that stuff," said Mrs. Foster. "I tried it for two weeks once, but didn't like it."

"Well, I thought I'd do it," said Mrs. Barker. "They're always needin' pickers, and you can go at your own speed. Why don't you come with me? I'll introduce you to Mr. George, the boss man."

Mrs. Foster laughed. "If I'd go to pickin' cotton, we'd be broke in two days' time. No, I'll let Big Abe catch fish and sell 'em and I'll take in the money."

"Is he aimin' to fish?" asked Mrs. Barker. "Here, at O'Donald Bend?"

"Yes," said Mrs. Foster. "We got a good place down under the river bank, below the store there. Abe'll put a sign out."

"Andy Dillard won't like that!" said Mrs. Barker.

"Who's Andy Dillard?"

Patsy came in just in time to hear what Mrs. Barker said.

"Andy's got a fish house down below us here, at the ferry landing. He sells to folks goin' back and forth to Tennessee on the ferry, and to the cotton pickers, too."

"Is there a store down there?" asked Mrs. Foster.

"It used to be a store and we ran it for a while," said Mrs. Barker. "*I* did it, Seth didn't help much. I sold soft drinks, peanuts, chewing gum and candy, maybe a few cakes and pies, but no beer. We're Christians and don't believe in it. I did that for a while, but didn't make out very well, so I quit."

"So it's a fish house now?" asked Mrs. Foster.

"Yes," said Mrs. Barker, "and Andy Dillard acts like he owns the whole Mississippi River. Don't say I didn't warn you!"

Mrs. Foster called the smaller children and they came running.

"Look, Mama," cried Patsy, pointing down the river bank. "Aunt Edie's got a whole yard full of chickens and a garden and a line for clothes down there. And look at her pretty flowers!" The window boxes on the houseboat were filled with red geraniums. "Aren't they purty?"

"They sure are," said Mrs. Foster. "I never was one to mess with flowers myself."

"They're no work," said Aunt Edie. "You just stick 'em in the ground and they grow."

"Not for me they don't," said Mrs. Foster. "They fold up and die."

A cat came up and rubbed against Mrs. Barker's leg. "Go away, Ten-Spot!" she said.

"What's the cat's name?" asked Patsy.

"Ten-Spot." Mrs. Barker laughed. "That's our ten-dollar cat!"

Mrs. Foster and the children stared. The cat did not have long hair, and it was not a Siamese, in fact it looked very common and ordinary. Its color was a mixture of yellow, white, gray and black.

"You don't mean to tell me you was a big enough fool to pay ten dollars for that . . . that skinny old alley cat!" exclaimed Mrs. Foster. "It looks like something somebody threw out in the dark!"

Mrs. Barker laughed.

"It's a ten-dollar cat all right," she said, "but we didn't buy it. A man borrowed ten dollars from Seth and left this cat, so he calls it his ten-dollar cat—Ten-Spot for short!"

"But if it's a *nice* cat," said Patsy, "it'd be worth ten dollars, wouldn't it?"

The women laughed.

"That's the kind you can't give away," said Mrs. Foster.

"I've tried a dozen times," said Mrs. Barker, "but it always comes back. It seems to feel at home here."

The children said good-bye to Aunt Edie and Mrs. Foster invited her to come for a visit. They started off, but Aunt Edie called them back.

"How long you folks goin' to be here?" she asked.

"Don't know," said Mrs. Foster. "Until we get a notion to move on, I reckon. It's a good place to lay and handy for the kids to go to school."

"Be sure to stay through cotton picking," urged Aunt Edie. She broke off some geranium slips and handed them to Patsy.

"Plant them in some dirt in tin cans and they'll grow," she said.

"They will?" asked Patsy, delighted.

As they walked back along the dusty road, Patsy said to Mama, "Aunt Edie's houseboat is *almost* a house, isn't it?"

"No more than ours is," said Mama.

"I mean it seems like a house 'cause it's up on land," said Patsy. "The water's way down at the bottom of the river bank, not up under the hull."

"Oh yes," said Mama.

As they passed the store, Patsy saw the girl Joella and her brother and little sisters sitting on the steps. The store was big and barnlike, sitting on high posts, so there were five steps up to the long entrance porch across the front. The girl waved to Patsy, but she did not wave back. She turned to Mama.

"That girl's always hangin' around that store," she said. "She must have a lot of money to spend."

"Maybe so," said Mama. "We'll find out soon enough."

The girl Joella and her brother and sisters followed Mama and the children down the river bank. As soon as Mama and Bunny went inside, Patsy put her slips down and she and Dan picked up stones and threw them. They chased the strange children up to the road. They called them names.

"I hope Mama didn't see us throw stones," said Patsy. "She made me give that girl a banana—only she didn't take it."

"They just better not come down our river bank again," said Dan.

Back at the houseboat, Daddy had his trotlines baited and was about to start off in the johnboat. Patsy went to the kitchen to look for tin cans to plant her geranium slips.

[104]

"Abe," said Mama on the porch, "Edie says there's a man down at Ashport Ferry Landing who has a fish house there and sells fish."

"That so?" said Daddy. "What's his name?"

"Andy Dillard," said Mama. "Edie says he won't like it if you try to sell fish here."

"What can he do about it?" asked Daddy.

"Run you out," said Mama. "Edie felt she had to warn you."

"Run me out?" Daddy laughed. "Just let him try it." He turned to Patsy. "Want to go with me, honey, to set my lines?"

"Yes," said Patsy, jumping in the boat.

On the way out toward the mouth of the chute, they passed the ferry landing, and saw the small ferryboat over on the Tennessee side. Patsy pointed to the Arkansas bank, where a small frame building stood. It had a sign on it, *Fish for Sale.*

"There it is," she said. "That's where Andy Dillard sells fish."

Daddy saw the sign and laughed, so Patsy laughed, too.

"There's plenty of fish in this old river for everybody," said Daddy.

But when they got back to the houseboat, a strange man stood on deck. Mama was there, too, talking to him. The man turned and waited for Daddy to get out of the boat. He was a large fat man with a red face and a tight-fitting cap. His ears stuck out at both sides and he did not look friendly. Patsy began to tremble. What did he want? How come he was standing on the porch of their houseboat with both his hands on his hips as if he owned it? As soon as he opened his mouth, Patsy knew that this was Andy Dillard and that Daddy was in for trouble.

[105]

"You can't tie up on this bank, mister!" said Andy Dillard in a loud blustery tone.

"Who says I can't?" Daddy's voice was soft and he had a half smile on his lips.

"*I* say you can't!" said the man. "My name is Andy Dillard. You can take your measly, fleabitten, ramshackle outfit away from this chute and go right back where you came from!"

Daddy began to go about his business on the fish barge as if he did not hear. After a while he said, "You own this river bank, do you?"

The man ignored his question. "I'm givin' you fair warning, mister," he said. "If you don't get out, I'll have the law on you."

"The law won't do a thing to me," said Abe Foster. "The Mississippi River is Federal Government property and I've got

an Arkansas fishing license. Want to see it?" He started to take it out of his pocket.

"No," said Andy Dillard. He spoke more quietly now. "I'm a friend of George Milburn. He owns this whole big cotton plantation and that's his plantation store. He said he didn't want any riffraff tied up to the river bank along here."

"The Federal Government's on my side," said Abe Foster with a smile. "I can tie up for sixty-five feet from the water's edge and nobody can put me off. If I tie a line up there and tear the bark off a tree, they can make me pay for it. I can drive a stake and tie up to it or to a tree 'for storm, delay or accident' and nobody can put me off. I can cut any wood that's not green. The Federal Government doesn't care. You'd better learn a little more about the law."

The man began to shout and bluster again. When he stopped to draw breath, Mama interrupted and said, "Supper's ready. Won't you set down and eat a bite with us, Mr. Dillard?"

"No! . . . No, thankee m'am!" the man said, stalking off angrily across the stage plank. He turned and glared at Abe Foster. "Remember I gave you fair warning!" Then he was gone.

When Daddy came in, he said, "Some things make me so mad, I could eat that fish barge!" But he did not mention Andy Dillard's name.

Patsy could not eat her supper that night. She leaned against Daddy's shoulder and said, "Is he gonna run us off, Daddy?"

"Of course not," said Daddy.

"How could he?" said Mama.

"I'll tell you what," said Patsy. "Let's buy a house. Then he can't run us off the bank. Let's buy a house up in town by the school."

"That's a good idea," said Mama, "but Daddy's got no money."

Daddy put his arm around Patsy and told her not to worry.

Dan told about the Parkers' ten-dollar cat and they all laughed.

CHAPTER VIII

A Visit to the Store

Nothing happened for a week. Then, on Saturday, Milly and Mama and Bunny went to town. They caught a ride at the corner by the store. That left Patsy and Dan alone at the houseboat. Daddy was busy with his nets and fishing gear.

"Gee, I wish I had a bike," said Patsy. "I'd take you on the back and ride up the river road all the way to Tomato."

"*Tomato!* That's a funny name for a town," said Dan.

"Mama said they had a store there once," said Patsy, "and they sold everything but one tomato. So they named the town after it."

"I don't believe that," said Dan.

"Let's go to the store here," said Patsy.

"And get candy," said Dan.

"We haven't any money," said Patsy.

"Let's ask Daddy," said Dan.

"Oh, he never has any," said Patsy. "He gives it all to Mama, and she took her purse with her."

"Well, let's go anyhow," said Dan.

"I've got an idea," said Patsy. "I'll take my eggs and sell 'em to the store man and then we'll have money to spend." She hurried to the kitchen and put half a dozen eggs her hens had laid into a paper sack.

"You takin' all of them?" asked Dan. "What'll we eat for breakfast?"

"Oh, the hens will lay some more," said Patsy. "I'll feed 'em good."

The children started up the river bank with the dog Blackie beside them.

"I hope those Harris kids won't be around," said Patsy. "We just won't give them a single bite of our candy."

"We'll chase 'em if we see 'em," said Dan, looking forward to a real fight.

But when they got up to the road, they forgot about the Harris kids.

"Look!" said Dan. "Daddy's sign is gone."

"Where was it?" asked Patsy.

"On the tree right here," said Dan. "I watched Daddy paint it and I came with him when he nailed it up."

"Are you sure it was on this tree?" asked Patsy.

"Yes, here's one of the nails still sticking in," said Dan.

"Where's it gone to—the fish sign?" Patsy's heart was beating so fast, she could hardly talk. "Do you suppose Andy Dillard came and took it down?"

"I don't know," said Dan. "It was there last night and now it's gone. Let's go tell Daddy."

"What's that over there?" asked Patsy, pointing to some bushes.

Dan went to look. "Here it is," he said. "It's chopped to pieces."

"Oh *no!*" cried Patsy.

Dan picked up the pieces and when they fitted them together it said FISH DOCK. They took them down to show Daddy.

Daddy said, "Put them down. I'll fix the sign and put it up again. Now you go and play."

Dan and Patsy went up the river bank again. Patsy still carried her eggs.

"I wish we had somebody to play with," said Patsy. "Somebody as nice as Ginny Cobb and the Cramer girls."

"I wonder where those Harris kids live," said Dan. "Maybe they would play with us."

"No, not after we threw stones at them," said Patsy.

"Maybe we could be nice to them," said Dan. "If they're the only kids around here, we got to have somebody to play with."

"Well . . ." said Patsy, "I s'pose they'd be better than nobody."

When they came to the road, there were the Harris kids again, as big as life. They always seemed to be hanging around the store. Why weren't they ever at home? Where did they live anyhow? They all had lollipops in their mouths and were sucking hard. They didn't even say *Hello.* Blackie yipped at them the way he did at strangers.

"They've got more money than we've got," Dan whispered to Patsy. "They can buy lollipops. I wish I had one."

"Lollipops is my favorite candy," said Patsy. "Come on, we won't look at them."

She and Dan hurried up the steps and went into the store. Blackie went in, too. The children had been in the store only once before, so now they took time to look around. It was nicer than any of the stores along the Mississippi River. It smelled good—a sort of cheesy-crackery-onion-harness-kerosene smell. It was more crowded than a dime store in a river town.

The children looked in the candy case and picked out the lollipops they wanted. Then they went to the storekeeper at the back counter. A short fat man was leaning on the counter talking.

Patsy asked the storekeeper, "You want to buy some eggs? Nice and fresh?" The man looked in her sack.

"Pretty small," he said. "Them your hens out there, runnin' all over the river bank?"

"They don't go far," said Patsy. "They always come home to roost."

The short fat man peeked into the egg sack, too. He winked at the storekeeper and said, "Mighty small, mighty small! They look more like hoot owl eggs to me! Reckon them hens got mixed up with some hoot owls?" The two men roared with laughter.

It made Patsy very angry. "Hoot owl, nothing!" she cried, closing her sack and starting away.

"Hey, come back if you want to sell 'em," called the store-keeper.

"If you make fun of my eggs, I won't sell 'em to you," said Patsy with dignity. "Come on, Dan."

"Aw, Patsy . . ." coaxed Dan. "I want some candy . . ."

But Patsy was out on the store porch by that time. Right there, leaning against the railing, all four of the Harris kids were standing, still sucking on their lollipops. It made Patsy jealous to see them.

Suddenly the big girl, Joella, called out, *"We* can have all the candy *we* want!"

"Huh!" said Patsy. "Who cares?"

"All we need to do is go right in and take it!" said Joella.

"That's *stealing!*" cried Patsy. "I'll tell the storekeeper on you. He'll put you in jail!"

All four children burst out laughing. They laughed and laughed and made Patsy and Dan feel very uncomfortable. They laughed so loud that Blackie started barking.

"You don't even know who the storekeeper is!" cried Joella.

"Well—who is he?" demanded Patsy.

"He's our *father!*" cried all the Harris kids together.

"Your *father?*" cried Patsy weakly.

"This is our father's store," said Joella. "He runs it for Mr. George, the boss man. He lets us have all the candy we want, and bananas too, when he gets 'em. That's why I didn't want one of yours."

"Where do you live?" asked Patsy in a chastened voice.

Joella pointed to the rear of the store, where several rooms were added on. "Right here," she said. "Right in back of the store."

Patsy and Dan looked at each other and felt very foolish. This made everything different. They wished now they had never thrown stones. Now they knew why the Harris kids were always hanging around the store. Patsy felt awkward. She did not know what to do next, but Joella did.

"Come on inside," said Joella, so they went back in the store.

When they came out, Dan and Patsy were each sucking a lollipop. And Patsy had a quarter in her pocket, which Joella's father had given her for the eggs. He even told her he knew they were real hen eggs. So Patsy felt better.

The lollipops made all the difference. The Harris kids were nice after all. Patsy and Dan would never throw stones at them again. Now they had somebody to play with.

[114]

When they started down the river bank, they saw that Daddy's fish sign was back up in its place on the tree. They wondered how long it would stay there. Dan showed the sign to Blackie.

"You be a good watch dog," he said. "If anybody comes to tear that sign down, bite a big hole in the seat of his pants!"

Blackie wagged his tail agreeably.

"Do you think Daddy will have a fight with Andy Dillard?" asked Dan.

"Oh—I hope not," said Patsy.

At first, O'Donald Bend had seemed a terrible place—with no house, no town, no friends—a terrible place to get away from. But now that Andy Dillard was trying to chase Daddy out of the chute, Patsy's whole feeling had changed. Now, and especially after she found out that the Harris kids were friendly, she wanted desperately to stay. That very day something else happened to strengthen this feeling.

In the afternoon, Joella Harris came down to see her. Joella's hair was combed, her face was washed and she had a pretty dress on. With her were two other girls. They said their names were Grace Eva and Brenda Collins and they lived up the road.

"Come on up to our house," said Grace Eva.

So Patsy walked with them up the river road toward Tomato. They passed the little abandoned one-room rural Bend schoolhouse. And the girls talked about what fun it was to ride the bus to school in town.

"What grade you in?" asked Joella.

"I passed to fourth," said Patsy.

"Oh, then you'll be in my class!" Brenda put her arm around

[115]

Patsy. "Will you sit next to me on the bus?"

Warmed by their friendship, Patsy could not tell them that the Fosters might not stay, that they might be forced by Andy Dillard to go off to some unknown place down river. All she knew was that Mama had said they would not return to Illinois.

The girls passed by cotton fields and sharecropper cabins and soon came to the Collins home. It was small and unpainted, with steps up at front and back. The steps were so high it must mean very high water.

"Does the river come way up here?" asked Patsy.

"Yes, in early spring," said Grace Eva. "Then we can't go to school. The school bus comes only to the levee and that's a mile back. So we just stay home."

Inside, the house was very plain, with three small rooms. There were beds in two rooms, and a wood stove, table and chairs in the kitchen. On the floor were patches of linoleum. The walls were papered with newspapers and there were no curtains at the windows. A few groceries could be seen in a cupboard. A water bucket and basin sat on a shelf outside the back door.

"Where's your mother?" asked Joella.

"She went in the truck to Cane Ridge to get water," said Grace Eva.

"Want a cold drink?" asked Brenda.

"Sure," said Patsy and Joella.

"Let's make Fruitade," said Grace Eva. "It won't be very cold, 'cause we don't have any ice, but it's good anyhow."

The girl took a pan, went down the back steps and filled it with water from a barrel that stood there. Brenda found an envelope

with pink powder in it. She poured the powder into the water
and stirred it with a spoon. Grace Eva took a cracker box from
the window sill and passed crackers around. Brenda poured the
Fruitade into glasses. It was lukewarm and oversweet, but the
girls drank it and said it was good. Then they went down the
steps and visited under the big oak tree.

The girls talked about how soon school would start. They
talked about the overcrowded school bus and laughed at the way
the boys and girls fought and pummeled each other on the way.
They talked about the good hot lunches served at the school.
Their eagerness for school to open made Patsy eager, too. Maybe
this school at Luxora would be all right. Maybe it would be as
good as the one at River City—or even better.

Then her new friends turned sad.

"Wish we didn't have to stay out so much," said Joella, "to pick that mean old cotton."

Grace Eva and Brenda agreed.

"They don't give us 'cotton vacation' any more at the town school, to let kids pick," said Grace. "So we just have to stay out."

"What do you pick cotton for?" asked Patsy in surprise.

"Oh, we get paid for it, we need the money," said Brenda.

"Our Daddy's a sharecropper," said Grace Eva, "so all of us have to help him get out his crop. Mama, too."

"Is it hard work?" asked Patsy.

Now the girls looked at her in surprise. "You've never picked any cotton?" they asked.

"No," said Patsy. "I don't know how."

"Why, where you been keepin' yourself?" asked Brenda.

"I lived on the river all my life," said Patsy, "until Mama put me in school in River City and we lived in a house there. I did three grades in two years."

Life on the river was something new to the cotton girls.

"And you never picked any cotton?" they asked.

Cotton was so much a part of their life, they could not imagine not knowing about it. It was a new idea to them that there were people in the world who did not pick cotton. They looked at Patsy in astonishment, as she shook her head.

"We'll show you how," the girls said laughing.

The Collins girls walked back with Joella and Patsy to the corner by the store.

"Want to see my houseboat?" asked Patsy.

[118]

"Oh, sure!" "Yes, yes. It sure looks nice," they said.

They went down the river bank and Patsy took them inside. The girls thought it was wonderful. They liked the bunk beds and Patsy promised to invite them to stay overnight and sleep in them sometime. They had never seen bottled gas before and were surprised when Patsy turned the burner on and it lighted itself from the pilot light.

Now for the first time Patsy saw her home with new eyes. How homelike it was with rugs and pretty curtains! Now she knew why Mama insisted on bringing her curtain stretchers all the way from Illinois. Patsy showed the girls the electric washer on the back porch, waiting to be hooked up to an electric wire from the post up on the road.

After the girls left, Patsy sat down on the leather couch. Even if it was only a houseboat, it was a very nice home. The Collins girls lived in a house on land, it was true. She felt sad when she thought of it. They had so little, yet they loved it, too. And they had to work hard picking cotton to help their father. She felt very sorry for them and wished she could help them. She was glad to have them for friends.

Then Mama and Milly and Bunny came back from town, loaded with sacks and bundles. They were all excited and happy because Milly had her mail-order package. It had been forwarded twice, but it had caught up with her at last. After the groceries, it took all of Mama's cash money to pay out the C. O. D. and the due postage. Milly put on her new dress with ruffled sleeveless blouse and full-gathered flowered skirt and flounced around, feeling very pleased with herself. She put a touch of rouge on her lips and new dime-store earrings in her ears.

"Don't you ever want to dress up and look *nice?*" she asked Patsy.

Patsy, dressed in T-shirt and shorts, stalked out in disgust.

"I should say *not!*" she shouted. "I'm going out with Daddy in his boat to set his lines."

Sunday was a very busy day. Uncle Seth and Aunt Edie came in their motorboat and took Mama and the children over to Fork-a-Deer Island to church. Aunt Edie was a Sunday School teacher there and had helped to start the church for the cotton farmers on the island. Daddy stayed at home and took care of fish customers all morning, and after Sunday dinner, they still kept on coming.

All week long Daddy had fished, setting his trotlines out at night and running them in the morning. While the river was low, he was still able to catch plenty of fish, some quite large. He held them in the fish box until Saturday and Sunday, ready for customers.

A tall young Negro man, dressed in Sunday clothes and wearing a straw hat, came down the bank and over the plank. He had a small boy with him, also nicely dressed. He glanced at the river and spoke to Mrs. Foster, who was sitting on the leather couch.

"Water's gonna dry up," he said.

"Yes, the river's fixin' to go away and leave us," said Mrs. Foster. "We had to push the houseboat away from the bank this morning."

"Got any catfish?" the man asked.

[120]

Abe Foster answered from the fish barge. "Might have one or two left," he said. The man and boy stepped over. "People been comin' since daylight. They been sittin' all over the bank, waitin' to buy fish. I'm about sold out. You gotta take any you can get."

Big Abe dipped a dip net into the fish box, pulled out several fish and dumped them on the floor of the barge. His feet were bare, the floor was wet and the fish flopped about in lively fashion. The man chose two.

"Watch out, mister!" cried the little boy. "The fish are biting your toes!"

"I'll quiet them," said Big Abe.

He knocked them on their heads with a hammer, then put them on the hanging scales to weigh them. He called the weights so Mrs. Foster could hear. "Four and a half pounds and one and a half," he said.

"They're thirty-five cents a pound," said Mrs. Foster. "A dollar ninety in all—I'll take the money."

"You're purty good at arithmetic," the man said as he paid her.

"I have to be," said Mrs. Foster. "My husband never went to school. Can't read. Can't figure, but he's just as smart as them that can."

Abe Foster spoke up. "I can too figure. I've got my own way of doin' it. If it's thirty five cents a pound, I figure one quarter and one dime for each pound. It's slow, but I can get it!"

The man laughed, and he and the boy went on.

Another customer, a stout, short man in new striped overalls came over the plank. He said he owned a restaurant and he wanted the biggest catfish he could get. Abe Foster went to look for it.

Patsy had taken off her Sunday dress and changed to T-shirt and shorts. She placed her six geranium plants in the sun on the deck and watered them carefully. They were already starting to grow.

As Daddy cleaned the fish, he threw the waste into the river. A dozen turtle heads soon popped up. More turtles crowded up around the houseboat. Patsy brought a dip net and tried to catch them. She was so absorbed in the turtles she paid no attention to the customers coming and going. She had a contented feeling, knowing that Mama was filling her purse up with cash money again, after spending it all the day before.

It was very hot in mid-afternoon, although there was a pleasant breeze on the river. Dan appeared with Joella's brother, whose name was Shorty, and several other boys he had found up the road. Back at the kitchen end of the boat, the boys put on their swimming trunks. Then they began to dive or jump off the guard into the river. They came up goose-pimply and shivering, and sat on the guard to get warm. Then Dan, who could not swim, rowed out in the johnboat and the other boys swam out to it and climbed in.

They were having a lot of fun, but Patsy paid no attention to them. She kept on dipping for turtles. She wanted to get a whole row of them, so she could play school. Suddenly, without any warning, she heard loud voices. She turned to look and her heart jumped into her mouth.

There was Andy Dillard on the river bank shaking his fist and shouting at Daddy. Was he coming over, and would there be a fight—on Sunday? What would Aunt Edie say? She had talked about fighting in Sunday School this morning and told the children how bad it was and said there were other ways to settle a quarrel. Daddy had a customer on the fish barge and wasn't even looking at Dillard. Was he coming over the plank to start trouble? Blackie knew something was wrong. He was barking loudly.

Patsy ran to Mama's side and clung to her in fright. Mama was standing up now, not saying anything either. Maybe it was better not to say anything. It would be pretty difficult to out-shout Andy Dillard.

"Let's go inside and shut the door," Patsy whispered to her mother. "Then we can't hear him."

But Mrs. Foster stood her ground.

Then Patsy looked and understood why Andy Dillard had

stopped on the river bank. The stage plank was down in the mud. He couldn't get over. Mama must have seen him coming and acted quickly. She must have unbolted the pin that held the stage plank and tossed the houseboat-end of the plank overboard. At least Andy Dillard could not come any closer. And he could not make the big jump of eight feet to get over to the fish barge.

But there was no way to stop his shouting. Even above Blackie's barking, they could hear his angry words.

"You can't sell fish here! You're ruinin' my trade, Abe Foster! You can't take my customers away from me. I got here first. Mr. George says he don't want no riffraff tied up here on the river bank! I'll have the law on you! I'll have the law on you!"

Andy Dillard kept on saying the same things over and over. Finally he stopped, out of breath.

Still Abe Foster said nothing in reply. He cleaned the fish for his waiting customer and weighed them.

But Mrs. Foster spoke up. "Let's not try to settle this on Sunday, Mr. Dillard," she said politely. "Come back tomorrow and we'll talk it over."

Andy Dillard went back up the river bank, blustering. At the top, he ripped Abe Foster's *Fish Dock* sign down from the tree and threw it angrily into the bushes. Then he drove off down to the ferry landing.

Mama watched him go. Then she told Daddy about the stage plank and he came and put it back in place. Mama did not talk about what had happened. She just said, "Go get the eggs and feed your chickens, Patsy."

Patsy started up the river bank with Dan and the dog. The other boys had finished their swim and gone home.

"Did you hear what that man said?" asked Dan.

"I'm not deaf," said Patsy.

"Is he going to run Daddy off the river bank?" asked Dan.

"He'd better not try it!" said Patsy fiercely.

CHAPTER IX

To Go or Stay

Big Abe Foster did not nail his sign up again and Andy Dillard did not come back the next day to talk things over. Abe Foster hoped that enough people knew now he had good fish to sell without the sign. He hoped they would keep coming, but they didn't. Several week ends passed without a single customer. Fishing was good and Abe Foster's fish box was so full he had to build a second one to hold the overflow. When the second one was full, he rented a truck and took a big load into Luxora and Osceola and sold them there.

He knew that Andy Dillard was taking all his trade, but what could he do about it? He and Mama talked things over.

[126]

"If I can't get customers," said Daddy, "I'll have to move on. We'll find another place, better than this."

"You'll let Andy Dillard run you off?" said Mama.

"What do you want me to do?" asked Daddy. "Go down there and punch his nose?"

"No," said Mama, "but there ought to be some way to work it out. I just kinda liked it here. There's Seth and Edie for friends, and Miz Harris up at the store, she's nice. And George Milburn, the boss man, will let us pick cotton for extra cash. Milly wants to pick to earn some spending money."

Patsy spoke up. "School starts next week, and I'm goin' to sit with Grace Eva on the bus."

"No," said Mama, "you'll have to sit with Bunny. Bunny's a big girl now, she's gonna start to school." Mama took the youngster on her lap.

"Oh, Milly can look after Bunny," said Patsy. "I'm goin' to sit with Grace Eva."

Daddy turned to go. "Better not start the kids to school here till we're sure we're goin' to stay," he said.

"Now look here, Abe," said Mama. "With all four kids of school age now, we've *got* to stay in one place during the school year anyhow. You can chase around up and down the river all summer if you want to, but these kids have got to have a chance to go to school. I don't want them to grow up like you did and not know how to read or write."

"How can I pay for their school supplies and clothes," asked Daddy angrily, "if I can't sell any fish?"

"Well, school's starting this week," said Mama, "so make

up your mind if we're goin' somewhere else or stayin' here."

"I wish I knew what that old sneak Andy Dillard is doin' to take my customers away from me," said Daddy. "I'll put up my sign again so the cotton pickers can see it. When they're picking, they've got money to buy. After picking stops, fish buying slows up."

It was Dan who found out what Andy Dillard was doing. He had arranged for his oldest boy, Chuck, to stay at the store corner, sometimes in the store, sometimes outside stopping cars. Chuck asked everybody, "Wanta buy catfish? Go to the fish house down by the ferry landing."

Chuck was about fourteen years old, big and strong, so Dan could not fight him.

Mrs. Foster did not know whether they were going or staying. But when school started, she went to town and enrolled the four children. They ran up to the corner by the store each day to catch the school bus. They all liked it except Bunny, who cried for Mama every day. Patsy sat with Grace Eva sometimes, or with Joella or Brenda. The bus was very crowded, and the children fought and threw books at each other just as the girls had predicted. They all thought it was fun until a boy got his head badly bumped. Then they quieted down.

One day the bus was not crowded any more. Cotton picking had started and the cotton children had to stay home to pick. Pickers came out in cars and trucks and could be seen all over the fields. The river road was a busy place now with all the coming and going. Sometimes the picking was in one field and sometimes in another. The Foster children and a few others were the only ones on the school bus until after it crossed the levee going back into town. Then Milly dropped out to pick cotton with Mama, because Daddy was making so little from fish. Mama needed cash money to get school clothes and supplies for the children.

The water in the river had been getting lower and lower ever since the Fosters came in August. Each day the wet mud strip on the bank grew wider, and the hard dry gumbo mud above it opened in wide cracks, wide enough to catch an unwary shoe or foot. Each day, the houseboat had to be pushed out farther from the bank to keep the hull in water. Abe Foster had to go farther and farther out toward the main river to catch his fish.

"That old river keeps on falling like somebody pulled a cork," said Mama.

Daddy laughed. "If it gets any lower," he said, "a turtle can soon cross over to Tennessee on dry land."

September was very hot and dry until a hard rainstorm came, then it turned cold. On Saturday as usual, the children wanted to go in swimming, but Mama said no. "You'll catch cold. I'm not going to pick cotton all week to pay doctor bills."

Daddy called Milly and told her to take Patsy and Dan to get grasshoppers for bait.

"Heck! That's no fun!" grumbled Patsy.

"I *hate* grasshoppers!" said Dan.

"They're about the only bait there is right now," said Daddy.

Mama gave the children glass jars with screw tops and they started out, with Blackie trailing behind. Milly tied a rag string around her jar and slung it over her shoulder. They went up the

[129]

river road to a soybean field. The vines were dry and dead and had turned yellow. The children walked back and forth snatch-ing at grasshoppers and putting them in their jars. It was fun for a little while, but the fun did not last long. Soon they got tired of chasing grasshoppers. Dan began to chase Patsy instead, and she stumbled and fell. She spilled her grasshoppers on the ground and she and Dan squealed as they tried to capture the jumping creatures again. Then they left their jars with Milly and ran back down to the store. There were no children around, so they went on down the ferry road. Blackie sniffed a rabbit and ran off and left them.

They came to a cotton field filled with pickers. Women and children dressed in sunbonnets and bunchy clothing, men and boys wearing straw hats were scattered over the field, dragging long white sacks behind them. A half-loaded cotton truck waited in the turnrow.

"Oh, there are the girls!" cried Patsy. "Let's go over."

Patsy and Dan crossed the rows and came up where the girls were picking.

"Come on, we'll show you how," said Grace Eva.

"Can I make a lot of money?" asked Patsy.

"Sure—if you get your sack full," said Brenda, putting the strap of her sack over Patsy's shoulder.

It wasn't fun at all. They all laughed at the way Patsy picked. They teased her and called it "goose-picking" and said she would starve to death. Patsy felt humiliated because the other girls were smarter than she.

"Aw, come on, Patsy," said Dan. "This is no fun."

They left the girls and went back to the road.

"I *hate* cotton picking," said Patsy. "I'd rather fish fish for a living."

"So would I," said Dan.

"Let's go to Aunt Edie's," said Patsy. "Maybe she'll give me a chicken. Aunt Edie's got lots more than she needs. I just want me a chicken *so bad*!"

They came to the lamplighter's houseboat, where red geraniums were blooming gaily in the window boxes. But the door was closed and there was nobody home. From the porch they could see another group of people picking cotton in a distant field.

"I bet Aunt Edie's over there pickin' cotton," said Patsy. "Let's go over there and see her."

"No," said Dan, "the boss man might make us pick. Let's go

down to the ferry. Maybe we could catch a ride."

"Oh no," said Patsy. "Andy Dillard lives down there. That's his fish house. See his sign, FISH FOR SALE? I wouldn't go there for anything. He'd run us off. He'd come out and cut our ears off!"

Dan laughed. "Don't be silly!"

"Well, I hate him," said Patsy. "I won't go near him, and that big boy, Chuck, he'll beat you up."

"There's Uncle Seth!" cried Dan. "Right down there by his boat. Let's go down and talk to him."

Without even stopping to look at the chickens in Aunt Edie's chicken yard, the children flew down the steep river bank so fast they could hardly stop at the bottom. There at a makeshift dock where several small boats and fish boxes were tied, Seth Barker was tinkering in his boat.

"When you goin' out, Uncle Seth?" cried Dan.

"I'm gettin' ready to go out on my run tomorrow," said Uncle Seth.

"Could you take us with you?" asked Dan.

Uncle Seth shook his head. "No kids allowed."

"Do you take all this stuff with you?" asked Patsy, looking at the things in the boat.

"Sure," said the lamplighter. "There's my slicker suit. If it rains, I got to keep runnin' my lights. If it's windy, it keeps the spray off. That's my post-hole digger and my wrecking bar and claw hammer. Then I take lamp wicks, one extra burner, and an extra globe and door glass—and an extra set of spark plugs. That can holds five gallons of kerosene. That's about all."

"How many motors you got?" asked Dan.

"Two outboard motors, one in and one out," said Uncle Seth. "I figure I've got three chances, with two motors just alike. If one breaks down, I put the other one on. If the second one breaks down, I can take the necessary part off the first one. I always carry extra spark plugs. I won't go on the river, even fishing, without extra spark plugs and sheer pins."

A cat appeared sniffing at Uncle Seth's fishing nets. Uncle Seth threw it a fish head. Patsy recognized it as the one she had seen at the houseboat.

"Is that your ten-dollar cat, Uncle Seth?" she asked.

"No," said the lamplighter. "He's a six-dollar cat now. That fellow came back and paid me four dollars of what he owes me. As soon as he pays the other six, it'll be just a plain tomcat."

The children laughed.

"Which way do you go?" asked Patsy. "Up river or down?"

"It all depends on the wind," said Uncle Seth. "The river is like the hallways of a house, with a breeze blowin' through and none at all up on the banks. You can catch more wind on the river than anywhere else. When it's thirty-five or forty miles an hour on land, it's too rough to be on the river. If the wind is comin' down river, I go up first. There's rough water on a downstream wind. If the wind is up river, I go down first and get rough water down there in an upstream wind."

"You sure do know the river, Uncle Seth!" said Dan.

"Not any better than Daddy does," said Patsy. "Daddy knows all about winds, too."

The lamplighter laughed. "Sure your daddy knows. He's been a river rat all his life."

"Do you go out every day, Uncle Seth?" asked Dan.

"Every fourth day," said the man. "The kerosene lamps will burn for five days. That gives me an extra day in case of a storm. I keep up with the radio on weather. When windy weather is predicted, I go out a day ahead. This throws an extra trip on me in a month, but it's better than risking my life in a storm."

"Gee!" said Dan. "You sure are a brave man, Uncle Seth. I'm gonna be a lamplighter like you when I get big."

"Fine!" said Uncle Seth. *"The main thing is to keep the lights burning and clean.* A lamplighter's got to be dependable. If a light goes out, it means some fool that's never been in a boat before might get drownded!"

"Bet you use lots of gas, don't you?" said Patsy.

"It takes twenty gallons a week for just my boats," said Uncle Seth, "and one quart of oil to every four gallons of gas." He climbed in his boat ready to go.

"Gee! I sure wish I could go with you," said Dan.

"Me, too," said Patsy.

"Can't take you out on my regular run," said the lamplighter. He picked up a lantern from the floor of his boat. "This lamp's broken and got to be replaced. I'm takin' the new one over to Island No. 27 light. Guess you can go along with me over there and back." He lifted a new lamp in the boat.

The children climbed in and soon they were chugging down the chute. At the ferry landing they saw children playing on the dock and in the water.

"Look, Dan, they're in swimming," said Patsy. "It's not too cold for *them*. Mama always says it's too cold for us."

"There goes the ferryboat over to Ashport," said Dan.

The ride around the south end of Fork-a-Deer Island did not take long. Uncle Seth climbed up the white ladder on the tripod, mounted the lantern and secured it, then opened the globe and lighted it. The children watched him and waited, then he climbed back down. Soon the boat was rounding the island again and going back up the chute.

"I'll let you out at the ferry landing," said Uncle Seth.

"O. K.," said Dan.

"Thank you for the ride, Uncle Seth!" the children called as they climbed out, and he started back to his own dock.

They waved good-bye and watched him go. Then they looked at the children playing in the river. An old boat was tied to a piling a little way out, and a small boy about five years old was playing in it. He had two sticks and was pretending to row. The other children were wading near the bank and splashing water on each other. The river bank was a sea of wet slimy mud. One boy picked up handfuls of mud and threw them at the other children. Suddenly he slipped and fell. When he picked himself up, he was covered with mud from head to foot. The others laughed and laughed.

Patsy and Dan stood at one side and stared.

"Who are they?" asked Dan.

"I don't know," said Patsy. "I never saw them before. They don't go to school on *our* bus. Maybe they're visiting somebody around here."

"Let's go home," said Dan.

Patsy looked up the ferry road. "Oh dear," she said, "why did we let Uncle Seth put us out here? Now we got to go past Andy Dillard's fish house and I'm scared. He might come out and . . ."

"I'm not scared," said Dan bravely. "He won't dare hurt us. I'll tell the boss man if he does."

In front of Andy Dillard's fish house, several cars were parked.

"Look at all the cars," said Patsy. "He's takin' all of Daddy's fish customers."

"We'll run by fast," said Dan, "then he won't even see us."

None of the children in the water had spoken to the Foster children. As they started to go, a loud scream rang out, so they turned back. A girl on the bank was pointing out to the old boat by the piling. Out there Patsy and Dan saw a small head just above water. They ran closer. Now all the larger children were

[136]

pointing and screaming, "He can't swim! He can't swim!"

Patsy looked and saw the little head go under. Then she saw it come up again. The next minute she was in the river with her clothes on. Her action was automatic. She was so used to jumping in, she did so without thinking. She swam as fast as she could to the old boat and got there just as the boy started going down for the third time. She dove under and grabbed his arm. She pulled him up, and steadying herself by holding to the boat with her left hand, placed the boy's limp arm around her neck. She had been rescued so many times herself, she knew just what to do. Then she swam back to the dock, dragging the boy along with her.

One of the strange children, a boy bigger than Dan, helped her lift the boy up on the dock. Patsy climbed up after him.

"Quick!" she said. "We've got to pump the water out of him."

She turned the boy over the way Stub Henderson had turned her over long ago at Mayfield Creek. She began pumping him up and down to expel the water from his lungs.

"Here! Let me do that!" a man's voice said.

It was Uncle Seth. He continued the artificial respiration and soon the boy stopped choking and could breathe again. The color came back to his face. The lamplighter had heard the commotion and, crashing through the bushes, had come as quickly as he could. The strange children, including the big boy, stood there like dummies.

"He's freezing—poor kid!" said Uncle Seth.

He took the half-drowned boy in his arms and hurried up the road to the place where the cars were waiting for the ferry to come back from Tennessee. The people, sensing disaster, crowded around Seth Parker in front of Andy Dillard's fish house. Patsy and Dan followed, but when Patsy saw Andy Dillard come out the door, she turned to Dan and said, "Let's run!"

Uncle Seth called her back.

"I'm cold," said Patsy, looking down at her dripping clothes. "I'm going home."

"Wait a minute," called Uncle Seth.

But Patsy and Dan did not wait. Looking back as they ran, they saw a woman come screaming out of the house to meet the people carrying the boy. They saw Seth Parker talking to Andy Dillard and they saw Andy Dillard pointing and shaking his arm in their direction.

"Look! He's coming! He's after us!" cried Dan.

[138]

"He can't catch us," said Patsy, breathless.

They ran up the road to the store and panted pell-mell down the river bank. The houseboat had moved out and lower down, beyond a wide stretch of wet mud. They flew across the planks laid in the mud and over the stage plank without stopping. They came face to face with Mama.

She stared at Patsy in her wet clothes. After one glance she began to scold.

"You fell in *again*? Accidentally or on purpose?" cried Mama. "I thought I told you it was too cold to go in the water today. Milly came back long ago with the grasshoppers. Where have you been?"

Patsy began to cry, so Dan answered briefly, "Down to see Uncle Seth. Then we went over to the ferry landing."

Patsy began to shiver and shake with the cold.

"Take those wet clothes off at once!" scolded Mama. "If you keep on fallin' in, Patsy, I tell you that old river's goin' to claim you one of these days. I always said you was my unluckiest one. If you could only get a little sense . . ."

Patsy was too tired to answer. She threw off her wet clothes and put on dry T-shirt and jeans. She was still shivering, so she jumped under the bed covers in the lower bunk. She fell asleep almost at once. After a while she was roused by the sound of men's voices. Dan crept in from the kitchen and whispered, "That mean old Andy Dillard's out there. He's come to run Daddy off the river bank. We'd better scram!"

Patsy and Dan tiptoed through the kitchen to the back porch. The stern of the houseboat was swinging out in deep water. It was too far out for them to try to jump from the guard to the land, and there was no plank. Besides, if they jumped, they would land in the sea of oozy mud.

"Here's the johnboat," said Dan, untying it.

"Let's go up the chute," said Patsy.

Patsy took the oars and they made good headway. Just before they rounded the bend, they heard Daddy calling. They looked back. He was on the back porch and beside him stood two other men and Mama. The children recognized Seth Parker and Andy Dillard.

"We got away just in time," said Dan.

"I know they saw us," said Patsy. "They'll come after us sure. I'll row as fast as I can and we'll find a place to hide."

When Patsy's arms got tired, Dan took the oars for a while. The chute up river was new to them, as Daddy always went down the chute to set his lines near the river itself. It looked like unexplored wilderness on both sides, with willows and brush coming down to the water. They saw no houses, no docks or landings on the banks and they wondered if no one lived there. They almost expected to see lions and tigers peeping through the bushes and monkeys hanging from the trees.

They were looking for a cove to hide in, when they came to an uprooted tree. A great mass of shaggy roots was upended. In the tangle of branches they saw a red johnboat floating.

"Look! There's a boat!" said Dan.

Patsy stood up. "It's a good one, too. There's hardly any water in it, so it doesn't leak much. Let's get it."

"It belonged to some man up river," said Dan. "I don't think he wants it or he'd a come after it."

Both children knew well the unwritten law of the river: Finders are Keepers. The river was looked upon as a storehouse of treasures. Anything might come floating down—planks, timbers, furniture, chests or boxes, ropes, baskets, boats. All river people were entitled to whatever they could salvage of the many strange things that the river deposited in their pathway.

"It'll be *our* boat," said Dan.

"Just yours and mine," said Patsy. "We won't let anybody else use it."

In the excitement over their find and in the hard work of freeing the red boat from the tangle of tree branches, the children forgot about Andy Dillard and the necessity of hiding from him. They pushed and shoved until they got the boat clear and out in the chute, where they tied it by a rope to their own johnboat. They took an empty pail and bailed the water out. They looked at

each other and grinned.

"It's a peach!" said Dan.

"It's *ours!*" said Patsy.

Then they heard the sound of a motor and there was Milly in Daddy's other johnboat. She yelled to them to tie on behind and they did. They tried to tell her about the red boat but she could not hear. In a few minutes they were back at the houseboat.

"Us kids found a boat," said Dan, jumping up on deck as they came alongside.

Patsy added, "Whoever finds anything in the river gets to keep it. So it's ours—Dan's and mine!"

"That's O. K.," said Daddy. "It's your boat."

Then Patsy gasped, for she saw that the two men were still there. She could not run now. She could not hide. She had to face them. She had to listen to what they were saying.

"All those big kids stood on the bank and yelled—those that didn't run away," said Seth Barker. "They was all cowards but her. I saw it all with my own eyes."

"What's her name?" asked Andy Dillard.

"Patsy," said Seth Barker.

Daddy and Mama stood back and said nothing.

"How old are you, Patsy?" asked Andy Dillard.

He wasn't cross at all. He spoke in a quiet, friendly voice.

"Nine, going on ten," said Patsy without looking up.

"Well—I don't know what I can do . . ." began Andy Dillard awkwardly. "She's a mighty fine girl." He turned to Daddy and shook hands. He kept pumping Daddy's arm up and down. "A girl to be proud of! A girl to be proud of!" He shook Mama's hand, too, and Patsy saw tears in Mama's eyes.

"We're sure glad you came by," Patsy heard Mama say. "Bring your wife along next time, I'd like to meet her."

Patsy could not believe her ears. Was Mama crazy or what— talking to Andy Dillard like that! Didn't she know he was Daddy's worst enemy?

It was Dan who was the brave one, Dan who insisted on a show-down. He marched up to Andy Dillard, shook his fist in his face and said, "You'd just better not try to run my daddy off the river bank," he said, " 'cause we're stayin' right here whether you like it or not."

Then Andy Dillard shook Dan's hand, too. He laughed and said, "I reckon there's plenty of fish in the river for your daddy and for me, too. And when I run out, I'll send my customers over to your dad."

He turned to Patsy and patted her on the back. "I'd like to give you a gold medal, Patsy," he said, "but I can't."

"What for?" asked Patsy.

"For pullin' that bad boy Bobby Dillard out of the river."

Patsy shrugged her shoulders.

"Oh, that!" she said. "That was *nothin'*!"

CHAPTER X

A Trip to Town

Patsy dipped her net in the fish box and brought up a large catfish.

"This here's a girl fish!" she said. "It's got lipstick on just like Milly! Look how red its mouth is."

The customer laughed, but Milly frowned as she cleaned the fish, weighed it and took the man's money. Milly sometimes waited on customers when Daddy was busy. After the man left, she tried to catch Patsy, but soon gave up. Nobody could run round the guards as fast as she.

Mama called Patsy and handed her the broom.

"Start sweepin'," she said. "This porch is just a catchall. Every-

[144]

body dumps everything here—shoes, boots, nets, fishing gear, boxes, boards, baskets, ropes, strings, clothes, wire, rubber tires, chicken feed and goodness knows what else. When they don't know where to put it, they dump it here." She picked up an armful and went indoors.

Patsy began to sweep lazily. It was fun to sweep for she never had to use a dustpan. She just swept all the refuse into the river so she would never see it again.

"There!" she cried, after one vicious swoop. "That's for you, Mister River. Take it away—you can have it."

Old newspapers, a cardboard carton and several rags went floating, then a roll of wire and some banana peelings. Blackie was sleeping in the sun, with Tom the cat curled up between his paws. Patsy swept carefully around them. She swept on and on,

dreaming. The Fosters were going to town that afternoon and she was trying to make up her mind what to get. *Swish!* went her broom. Then she looked in dismay. There were her shoes floating in the river, one like a boat and the other upside down. Quickly she dropped her broom, fell flat on the deck and stretched out her long arms, but she could not reach them. She ran and got a fish pole and tried to reach them with that. But the current was a lively one, and already the river was taking them away from her.

Patsy jumped up and said to herself, "Well, I'll just give them to some little old girl down river!" She went on sweeping.

"You know what," Patsy called to Mama inside, "at the Harrises' store they're selling watermelons for fifteen cents."

Mama was not interested in watermelons. Mama was talking to Milly.

"There's one job I hate," Mama said. "I've got to wash their heads every Saturday. Good thing it rained yesterday—I've got a whole tubful of nice clean rainwater. Come here, Bunny."

"Dan has two nickels in a big glass jar with a screw top," said Patsy. "It's up on the shelf over his bed."

No reply from Mama.

"I'm savin' my money," said Dan.

"He's savin' it to spend it, Mama," Patsy went on.

No reply from Mama.

"If Dan had another nickel, he could buy a watermelon for all of us to eat!" said Patsy.

This time Mama heard.

"I told you you can't buy a watermelon," she said. "I told you it would give us all the thirty-day chills. Eatin' watermelon so late in the season always gives people the chills."

On the back porch, Mama started the head washing. Milly was done already and had hers up in pin curls. Bunny sat on a box, leaning over, her eyes covered with a washcloth. Mama rubbed the little girl's head vigorously, soaping it well. Bunny did not cry or fuss.

"Don't you go away, Patsy," called Mama. "You're next."

"No," said Patsy, "Dan's next."

Just then Daddy came out.

"Can't leave the houseboat settin' on this mudbank," he said. "Time we get back from town, the river'd have run plumb away and left us. Then we'd be settin' purty."

"What you goin' to do?" asked Mama.

"Shove her off into deep water," said Daddy.

"Again?" asked Mama. "Right now when I'm washin' heads?"

Daddy nodded. "Radio says the river'll keep on droppin'. We should a moved off the mud sooner."

Daddy brought a long plank with a rope on it and threw it out to the bank. He got on the plank and with a long spike pole tried to push the houseboat away. But it did not move. Patsy jumped in the johnboat, started the motor at its stern, and soon it was running full blast and churning up the water. Milly and Mama helped Daddy push on the long spike pole, but still the houseboat did not move.

"Wait," said Daddy.

The others sat down while he went to the front porch, let the stage plank down and pushed the front part of the hull off the muddy bank. There was more water around the hull there, so it was easier. He pushed till the bow was well out in the water.

Mama called to Patsy, "What you doin' out in that boat? You come and help us here."

"Doin' what?" asked Patsy.

"Pushin', pushin', just pushin'."

"Daddy wants me to push with the johnboat," said Patsy.

"Oh yes," said Milly, "you like to get out of anything that's real hard work."

"That's right." Mama laughed. "There's Patsy, the dog and the cat. That's three no-count things. That girl's no river rat, even though she *was* born in the Mississippi River."

"Yes, I am, too, a river rat," said Patsy. "I got a gold medal for lifesaving!"

"Ha, ha! Like heck you did!" teased Milly.

When Daddy came back to the stern, Mama told him, "You ought to get a man or two to do this pushing."

"We can make it now all right," said Daddy. He called to Patsy and told her to shove with the motor boat as soon as they pushed.

"I can help—let me!" said Dan.

"You get on the bank," said Mama. "You're just so much excess weight. You're too skinny for this kind of a job."

Dan laughed. "Want me to jump and land in the mud?"

"Now PUSH, everybody!" shouted Daddy.

Mama and Milly and Daddy pushed on the spike pole, but Patsy was looking the other way.

"Patsy!" yelled Daddy. "The motor!"

Patsy pulled the string and the motor started with a loud roar. Blackie began to bark. With the combined pushing and shoving of the whole family, the hull was dislodged from the mud and it slid into the water. Mama and Milly sank back exhausted.

"Shut off the motor, Patsy!" yelled Daddy.

She was out in mid-river going in circles, with the motor still running full tilt.

"That girl!" cried Mama. "She gets to chewin' on that chewin' gum and lookin' around at the scenery, and forgets to shut the motor off."

"You gonna wash my hair, Mama?" asked Patsy when she came in.

"There's not time now," said Mama, "if we're goin' to town." Mama had picked cotton during the week, even though she hated it and was a slow picker, and now she had ten hard-earned dollars in her purse. "We must be ready when Aunt Edie comes by for us in her car."

"Goody! Goody!" cried Patsy. "My hair's not dirty anyhow."

"Patsy doesn't even know if her hair's dirty or not," said Milly.

"Now hush, you two," said Mama. "Go get yourself cleaned up, Patsy. You, too, Dan."

Daddy sat on the rear deck, hung his feet over and washed them in the river. Then he went to the wash bench and washed arms, neck and face with the washcloth. He shaved at the old washstand to the left of the door. It had a small mirror hanging over it. When he went to put on his shoes, he said, "Ouch! Goin' to town in shoes makes my feet burn like fire!"

Mama and Patsy washed and dressed in the bedroom. Mama combed Patsy's hair and tied a ribbon round it. She herself put on a navy blue dress with a white collar. Patsy hunted and hunted in the rack of dresses on the wall and finally chose a pretty blue dress with pink flowers. She found her blue sweater and put it on.

Up on the road, a car horn sounded.

"That's Aunt Edie!" cried Mama. "Everybody ready?"

"Can I go with you, Mama?" begged Bunny.

"No, you be a good girl and stay here with Milly," said Mama. "I can't fool with you. Patsy and Dan are bad enough."

"Buy me some candy then, Mama," said Bunny.

Just then Patsy came out on the porch. Mama looked her over from head to foot.

"Where are your shoes?" she asked. "You can't go to town barefoot."

"Well . . . er . . . I . . ." began Patsy, halting. "They're no good anyway, they don't hardly fit me any more.'' She paused. ''They're about the right size for Bunny . . . Buy me some shoes, Mama.''

''WHERE are your shoes?'' asked Mama again.

It was hard to tell Mama that her shoes were going down river like little lost boats seeking new homes on some other little river girl's feet. Mama would not understand that.

''Well . . .'' Patsy began, ''you know how things are always rolling off the porch . . . and how when you drop anything . . . it just *jumps* into the water of itself . . . and you know how that old river keeps goin' and goin' and goin' and never stops but takes everything along with it . . .''

Beep, beep, beep sounded the horn of Aunt Edie's car, more insistently than ever.

''That's enough, Patsy,'' said Mama. ''Why can't you say right

out that you threw them in the river? We mustn't keep Aunt Edie waiting . . ."

Daddy was already halfway up the bank, with Blackie following. Mama started over the stage plank with Dan just ahead.

"I didn't *throw* them . . ." said Patsy. "They practically *jumped!*"

"What with you and the dog and the cat . . ." said Mama, leaving her sentence unfinished. She started on saying, "Milly, call the dog back."

"Buy me some shoes, Mama," said Patsy. "I didn't *throw* them in, I just *swept* them in by accident. They got right in front of my broom and I didn't notice it until they were in the river. I didn't mean to do it."

"If you'd stop your dreamin', you'd get along a lot better," said Mama. There was no time to scold the girl now.

Then they were in the car driving past the cotton fields, some still white with unpicked cotton, over the levee and down the gravel road to Luxora. But they did not stop there. They kept on to Osceola. *If I'd a known we was goin' to Osceola,* said Patsy to herself, *I'd a saved my shoes. I don't want the people in Osceola to see me walkin' barefoot. But maybe then Mama will have to buy me new shoes.* She cheered up at the thought.

"Buy me some shoes, Mama," she said aloud.

"If the fish don't run better, you'll go barefoot all winter," said Mama."

"Oh no, you picked cotton last week, Mama," said Patsy.

"Daddy needs a new shirt and Dan needs overalls and shirts and a haircut," said Mama. "And I got to get food enough to last us a week. You'll have to wear those old shoes of Milly's—they're about your size now."

Daddy left them to get gas and the things he needed for his boats. Mama went first to the supermarket and she and Aunt Edie came out loaded with sacks of groceries. They headed back to the car to leave them.

The streets were crowded with cars, and the sidewalks with people. All the cotton pickers had been paid off in cash and had come to town to spend their money. Family groups, parents with children from babies to teen age were everywhere. Men and boys were leaning on the hoods and fenders of parked cars and trucks, talking.

To Patsy, it seemed a year since she had set foot on a sidewalk, and the cement felt hard to the soles of her bare feet.

"Buy me some shoes, Mama," Patsy kept saying until Mama told her to hush.

In her own mind, Patsy was trying to decide what kind to get. She was thinking how nice a pretty pair of red shoes would be, thinking so hard she did not watch where she was going—until she was brought up sharp by a loud scream and a screech. Mama did the screaming and the car, a strange car that appeared from nowhere, did the screeching when it stopped within six inches of Patsy's bare feet. Dan came rushing up to pull her back to the sidewalk. Patsy had somehow gotten out into the middle of the street without realizing it.

A policeman came running over and spoke to Mama in a loud voice. Mama dropped one of the sacks of groceries and Dan had to pick everything up from the sidewalk. Strange people crowded round on all sides, pushing and staring and talking. Mama was really upset.

"What's the matter?" asked Patsy.

"Matter?" cried Mama. "That car nearly ran over you!"

"She walked right out in front of that car, Mama," said Dan, "and made the man stop."

"Heck!" said Patsy. "He's got brakes!"

"Now Patsy," said Mama, "you're not on the river. You're on a street in town, and the cars are not going to go around you. I see I'll have to show you how to cross a street."

"I can show her how, Mama," said Dan. "Look, Patsy, there's a red light. That means we've got to wait till it turns green. We only cross over when it's green."

"I didn't know they had buoys in town," said Patsy, grinning.

Mama turned to Aunt Edie. "That girl's lived too long on the river," she said. "You never saw a worse greenhorn in town."

A large man who had been standing by, laughed out loud.

"What a girl!" he said. "Smart on the river, but not so smart in town!"

They turned and saw that it was Andy Dillard.

"I've warned her about the river, Mr. Dillard, but not about cars," said Mama.

Patsy spoke up, "Buy me some shoes, Mama."

Andy Dillard looked down at her bare feet. "She needs shoes?" he asked.

Mama nodded, laughing. "Fish don't bite fast enough to keep four kids in shoe leather!"

"You come with me, Patsy." Andy Dillard took her by the arm and started to cross the street on a green light.

Patsy looked up in alarm. All her old fear of the man returned.

"Where you takin' me?" she asked.

"You go right along with Mr. Dillard, honey," Mama said.

A half hour later, when Andy Dillard and Patsy came out of the shoestore, Patsy was wearing white socks and new shoes. The shoes were red strap sandals. They pinched her toes, because she had gone barefoot all summer and fall, but she did not mention it. She knew now why Daddy hated shoes and said they made his feet burn like fire. She did not mention it because hers were the most beautiful shoes in the town of Osceola and the state of Arkansas, if not in the entire United States of America.

Mama and Aunt Edie and Dan all thought the red shoes were very nice. Patsy saw some strange girls looking at them, too, so she felt very proud. They all thanked Mr. Dillard who said it was nothing.

"I just wanted to do something for her," he said modestly, "since I couldn't give her a gold medal." He turned to Patsy. "Will you be careful now crossing the streets in town?"

"Oh, yes, Mr. Dillard," said Patsy sweetly and softly. "I'd hate to be run over with my new shoes on." She gave him her sweetest smile and for the first time accepted him as a friend.

On the way home, Daddy said, "Let's go by the river and see how it looks."

"It looks the same as it always did," said Mama.

"Let's take the river road, Edie," said Daddy. "I want to see what the river looks like to land folks."

"You afraid it might change its mind and start runnin' upstream?" asked Aunt Edie.

"No," said Daddy. "But take me off this river for even half a day and I'm lost. I just can't be satisfied to save my soul!"

Aunt Edie laughed and drove along the river road. She stopped at gaps in the willows through which the river could be seen.

"When I was workin' in that factory up there in Detroit makin' big money," said Daddy, "I could shut my eyes, imagine I had a line on such and such a point and was catchin' me a great big catfish! I could just *see* it—even when I was poundin' metal all day long."

"You're a sad case!" Mama laughed.

"I can't help it," said Daddy. "Even to go to town for half a day makes me downright homesick for that old river."

"But Daddy," said Patsy, "town is *nice!* With all those stores!"

"The river is better," said Daddy.

[156]

When they got home Patsy changed clothes and skinned the cat on the porch rafter.

One day the next week Patsy went over to Fork-a-Deer Island with Daddy and the dog Blackie to get grubworms. With the coming of cooler weather, it was too late for grasshoppers, so Daddy had to change bait to something new. He took his double-bitted axe with him, came to an old hollow log and split it open. Inside was a nest of fifty or seventy-five grubworms, that would, if undisturbed, turn into horseflies. He started to pick them up.

"Here, take these!" Daddy gave Patsy a handful of the fat white squirming worms. "Put them in the bucket. They won't hurt you."

Patsy took them in her hand, but before she found the bucket, she screamed. "They bit me! They bit a piece right out of my finger!"

Daddy laughed. "You must have squeezed them too hard."

Patsy brought the bucket over. "You can put them in the bucket yourself."

Blackie ran sniffing around in circles, yelping.

"Oh, look! Blackie's after a rabbit," said Patsy. "Go get a rabbit for our supper, Blackie!"

Daddy went from one log to another and also split open some rotten stumps. Soon he had the bucket nearly full. "Come here, Patsy!" he called.

There in the hollow of a log was a snake about eighteen inches long.

"Look at this purty snake," said Daddy.

Patsy thought it was pretty, too. "It looks just like peppermint candy, with red stripes going round and round, but I guess I won't eat it! Don't kill it, Daddy. Let it go."

They watched the snake slide off and disappear under the fallen leaves.

The sun was warm on the island bank when they went back to the johnboat. Blackie came up panting and exhausted, minus a rabbit.

"This seems to be our day for snakes," said Daddy, looking up.

Patsy ducked. Over her head, draped over the branch of a tree, was a long brown water snake with reddish undersides spotted red and black.

"It's all ready to drop in the water to catch a fish or a frog," said Daddy.

"Just so it doesn't drop on me," said Patsy.

"Don't you want it for a pet?" asked Daddy.

"No!" said Patsy. "Mama won't let me have snakes. Don't you

[158]

remember she dumped that king snake of mine in the river? But I would like a turtle. I just want me a turtle so bad—a great big old one, not one of those teeny dirty mud turtles. Can't you find me a snapper, Daddy?"

"A snapper!" Daddy laughed. "You don't know what you're talking about, girl. In all the trips I've made up and down this old river, I've never seen a snapping turtle. They stay deep down in the mud at the bottom of the river or in a dried-up slew. You wouldn't want one of those fellers. They're mean—they'll take right after you in the boat. They weigh forty or fifty pounds, and they got a regular hawk bill and horns on their back."

Back at the fish barge, Daddy poured boiling water on the grubworms in the bucket.

"That'll make 'em tough," he said, "so the shrimp can't bite 'em off. That'll give the fish a chance at them."

Patsy sat down and helped him bait his hooks. It took a long time because there were over six hundred grubworms. Patsy counted them. After the hooks were baited, she went out with Daddy to set his lines. She always enjoyed the river on her trips alone with Daddy. By nightfall it had turned chilly, so it was good to get back to the houseboat again.

Inside, it was warm and cozy. A wood fire was burning in the little cast-iron stove, and Mama was making sorghum cakes for supper. A man who had a sorghum mill on the island had brought some molasses to the store and Mama had bought a gallon. She mixed a batter and poured sorghum molasses in. She cooked the batter in a big skillet like cornbread. When it was done she mixed a second batch.

"Goody, goody!" cried Patsy. "I smell sorghum cakes!"

Milly and Dan and Bunny came up sniffing, too.

"I can never make enough," Mama told Daddy. "These kids would eat a washtubful. They really like 'em!"

"No wonder," said Daddy. "They're all empty clean down to their toes."

Tom the cat came up meowing and Blackie the dog tugged on Daddy's pants' leg. They were both hungry, so they had to have their share.

Mama spoke to the pets. "You both belong to this outfit," she said. "You're worse than the kids, the way you like sweets. I never knew a dog and cat with a sweet tooth before."

When everybody was full of sorghum cakes and the other children had left the table, Patsy put her arm around Daddy's shoulder.

"Now that Andy Dillard's our friend," she said, "we're stayin' right here at O'Donald Bend, aren't we, Daddy?"

"It all depends on how the fish keep bitin'," said Daddy.

"Andy Dillard says there are plenty of fish in the river for you and him, too," said Patsy.

"Sure," said Daddy, "if you can catch 'em. Cold weather's comin' soon. I can't fish trotlines after it's cold. Gotta get my hoop nets out. Gotta knit some new ones."

"If you catch lots of fish," Patsy went on, "then you'll get us a house, won't you?"

"A house?" said Daddy. "You hankerin' for a house again? What's the matter with this houseboat? It's a sight better than these little old shacks the sharecroppers live in. I thought you was a borned houseboat girl. What's the matter with the river, I'd like to know?"

"Nothing," said Patsy. "It's still the same old river. But I'd like a house up on the river bank. I wouldn't want to be *a long ways off* from the river, you understand . . . I'd like it to be where I could look out the windows and see it sometimes . . ."

Daddy laughed and laughed. "Spoken like a real river girl!" he said. "She wants to get away from the river, yet she don't want to get away from it. The river's in your blood, girl. You just can't help it."

"Oh no," said Patsy. "My blood's not all river. I like town, too."

"You're just not town-broke," said Mama with a laugh. "Anybody that doesn't know how to cross a street on a green light!"

"Couldn't we get a house up on the river bank?" asked Patsy again.

"Now, Patsy," said Mama. "you stop naggin' your daddy. He's tired tonight. When that girl sets her mind on something she wants, she won't give a body peace until she gets it. Of all my kids, she's the nagginest!"

"Your mother's right, Patsy," said Daddy. "Stop your nagging."

"It's only a house I want," said Patsy. "A house on the river bank."

"A *house!*" scolded Mama. *"Only* a *house*—as if we was livin' in a tent, I s'pose."

"If we stay here all winter," said Daddy, "we'll get up on the river bank all right."

"We will?" cried Patsy eagerly.

"The river will take us up and set us right down whether we want to go or not," said Daddy.

"Just wait till high water comes long about February," said Mama.

"High water?" asked Patsy.

"That's when the people in *houses* get in trouble," said Daddy, "even the people with their houses set high on stilts like all those up the river road to Tomato. But high water's no trouble to a shantyboater. He's not anchored down to one spot. He just goes up and down, up and down as the river goes. So he's perfectly safe."

Patsy looked out the window at the high mudbank rising from the shallow river. The houseboat was so low now, she could not see any sign of store or road above. It was hard to imagine that the houseboat would be lifted all the way up there on a rising river. What a terrific amount of water it would take to fill that great deep river valley!

"Wait till the winter snows melt up there in the north and all that water comes pouring down the Ohio, the Missouri and Mississippi rivers!" said Daddy. "We'll get up on top of the river bank all right!"

"Oh goody!" cried Patsy. "Up on *top* of the river bank! I can hardly wait!"

CHAPTER XI

A House for Patsy

Patsy and Dan appeared on the river bank, pulling something behind them.

"What's that you got?" asked Daddy.

"It's a Christmas tree," said Patsy. "Dan and I got it in the woods. Tomorrow's Christmas. You'll have to move those nets, so we can get in."

Daddy shook his head. "Can't move them till I get done."

"We'll set it up in the living room, Dan," Patsy said.

She started across the stage plank, but Daddy's great hoop nets on hoops four feet in diameter, covered the entire porch and blocked her path. She and Dan sat down on the stage plank to wait.

[163]

"Daddy's in the knittin' business," said Mama. "Don't bother him now."

Mama sat in an easy chair with a warm coat on, untangling a great mass of twisted Nylon fish cord.

"This stuff has got into nine hundred and ninety-nine knots," she said. "Nylon is terrible, it tangles so bad."

"But it will last ten times as long," said Daddy. "That acid in the river water eats the cotton lines up in no time."

"I'd rather sew on my quilts," said Mama. "When I'm shut in all winter long, I don't do a thing but piece quilts. I want to get that Flower Garden done soon . . ."

Abe Foster was busy knitting hoop nets for winter fishing. His wooden shuttle moved briskly in and out. Seven large hoops were already joined together with a knotted crisscross netting. Now he was working on two "throats"—narrow openings where the fish could go in but not get out. He hung the tail of the net to a porch rafter and let the hoops fall.

"They're purty," he said, looking at his handiwork, "when you get 'em done without any tar on 'em. They're even purty after they're tarred. Not everybody can build a nice net like that! Andy Dillard buys his ready-made, but he can have that kind. I wouldn't give fifteen cents for a ready-made net."

"But, Daddy, our Christmas tree!" cried Patsy impatiently. "We got to set it up and get it trimmed."

"Where you goin' to put it?" asked Mama.

"Inside—in the front corner by the window," said Patsy.

"It's too hot in there," said Mama, "with the heater so close. All the needles would fall off before night."

On the porch where the old leather car seat had sat as a couch all summer, a barrel of oil had been placed on wooden horses. A pipe from the barrel ran under the hull and through the floor in the front room to feed the heater. Although the houseboat walls were only of wallboard covered with wallpaper, the rooms stayed cozy and warm, helped by the heat of the sun on the flat roof and the wood fire in the little cast-iron stove in the kitchen.

"Your mama keeps it hot enough inside to roast the cat!" said Daddy. "I can't stand it to come indoors hardly."

"But where can I put the tree then?" asked Patsy.

"Out here on the porch will be better," said Mama.

"But there's no room," said Patsy. "Look at all the junk. Look at those big old hoop nets of Daddy's. Why does he have to build nets on Christmas?"

"We have to eat on Christmas, too, honey," said Mama. "Let's see how big your tree is."

Dan stood it up on the stage plank and they looked at it.

"It's not very big . . ." said Mama doubtfully.

"It's the biggest one we could find," said Dan. "I chopped it down myself."

"It looked lots bigger out in the woods," said Patsy.

"I'll tell you what you can do," said Mama. "Do you want to put electric lights on it?"

"Oh yes! We do!" cried Patsy and Dan.

"I think I brought that old string of lights from River City," said Mama. "Let's put the tree up on the electric washer, right at the corner there, where everybody can see it, fish customers and all. Then you can plug the light cord in at the washer outlet."

"Goody! Goody!" cried the children. "Oh, how pretty that will be."

After it was decided that the Fosters were staying in O'Donald Bend for the school year at least, Daddy brought an electric wire from the pole up on the road to the houseboat. So they stopped using the kerosene lamps and had bright lights to see and read by, and Mama was able to use her electric washer. It had been brought from the rear to the front porch. Mama still heated her water in the iron kettle over a wood fire on the bank. But it was handier for her to carry it and put it in the washer on the front porch, instead of going around on the guard.

The river had been gradually rising since November with the fall rains, so the houseboat was now about halfway up the bank. Daddy finished his knitting, hung his hoop nets out of the way

and built a base for the Christmas tree. Patsy hung a few shiny balls on it, plugged in the light cord and Dan turned the switch on. The tree looked very pretty with its bright sparkling lights shining in the darkness.

Patsy and Dan ran up to the road and said they could see it plainly from there. On Christmas day a heavy snow came and laid a carpet of white over everything—over the mud bank and assorted fishing gear, over the great flat roof of the houseboat, over the boats tied by the porch and over the bare branches of the trees on the river bank. Aunt Edie and Uncle Seth came down to dinner and Mama roasted a duck that Daddy had shot over on the island. There were presents for the children and everybody had a happy time.

On Christmas afternoon Daddy had to run his nets as usual. Patsy went with him in the johnboat down to the end of the chute. The long line of hoops connected by nets hung sideways in the water, near the bottom of the river. On one end of the long line was a weight to act as anchor, on the other end a bottle buoy to float. Daddy raised the first hoop up and rolled the net up on the boat. He shook the fish forward and dumped them out in the bottom of the boat.

"Oh, look at that big tow coming!" cried Patsy. "Remember that crazy pilot who nearly busted into our houseboat up at New Madrid and broke all our ropes?"

"I sure do," said Daddy. "A good pilot can steer a line of barges through the eye of a needle, but here they can't take them around a bend without hittin' somebody."

"I'll never forget that towboat," said Patsy. "The cook had

[167]

a great big bunch of bananas hanging out on deck. I was wishin' that old towboat would sink, so you and me could go out and get those bananas!"

Daddy laughed. "You're some banana girl!"

The towboat was coming up river fast. The barges were filled with green sulphur loaded high as a house, to be used in making steel and glass. Daddy and Patsy watched the outfit come closer and closer. Daddy's distant sight was unusually good.

"It looks like the *Bessie P* to me," he said. "Golly, I do believe it is the *Bessie P!* I haven't seen Captain Leonard for a coon's age. He's bought fish from me many and many a time."

"Why, the tow is slowing up, Daddy," said Patsy.

Daddy started his motor and went closer. Suddenly he heard a man's friendly voice, magnified over a loud speaker. "Got any turtles today, Big Abe?" The voice was so loud it could be heard for five miles.

Daddy slapped his knee in delight. "It *is* Captain Leonard sure as shootin'! He's the turtle-eatin'est man ever I did see! Look, he's stopping the tow . . . he's not supposed to do that, but he's an old friend! Imagine him spottin' me clear across this old river, and callin' me by name! We'll go over and see him."

The towboat waited until Daddy came alongside. Several deckhands looked down from the barges and grinned. Captain Leonard wanted all the turtles he could get. Fortunately the haul of the hoop nets had brought up half a dozen. Daddy loaded up the basket the cook let down on a rope. Daddy and the captain talked and reminisced. When the basket came back down it held a surprise—apples and oranges and a huge stalk of bananas.

"*Bananas!*" cried Patsy. "Look at all the *bananas!*"

"This here's my *banana* girl!" Daddy told Captain Leonard. "Patsy will do most anything short of sinkin' a towboat and goin' to jail to get herself a bunch of bananas!"

The men talked and then the captain asked, "Did you ever eat any deer meat, Big Abe?"

"No," said Daddy. "Rabbit's more my style, and the island's full of them. When the fish don't bite, we eat rabbit. My wife says we've eaten so many this winter, she thinks we'll soon all start hopping!"

The captain spoke to the cook who tossed down a hunk of venison. "Try it on the kids!" he said. "I think you'll like it! Merry Christmas!"

Soon the *Bessie P* began to move again, while Daddy and Patsy watched from a safe distance. What a surprise it was to bring all the fruit to the other children. Daddy hung the stalk of bananas to the rafter beside the Christmas tree.

"Don't make yourselves sick eatin' bananas," said Mama.

Winter had come now in earnest. With melting snows in the north, the Mississippi River rose higher and higher, taking the Foster houseboat with it. Up, up it went past the old campfire where Mama used to heat water and wash her clothes, past the trees where Patsy's hens' nests had been nailed for so long, past Mama's clothesline and the big iron vat where Daddy tarred his hoop nets, past the open space where Aunt Edie used to park her car and on up to the road. Each day the plunder on the bank had to be moved higher—the chicken coop, washpot, the piles of

driftwood, old baskets, nets, hoops, salvaged planks, scraps of
iron and assorted junk, all the things that might come in handy
some day.

In January it snowed again. One day when Patsy came running
from the school bus, she slipped on the snow on the stage plank
and fell into the water with a great splash. She got her jacket,
jeans and boots wet and muddy.

"Well!" Mama put her hands on her hips and looked at her.
"Some one has to go in now and then," she said, "to let us know
how cold the water is."

Milly teased. "Patsy got a gold medal for lifesaving, but she
can't save herself!"

Dan helped pull her out and Bunny helped her take her boots
off. Blackie came up and licked her face, and after she put on
dry clothes, Tom the cat jumped into her lap to cuddle there.

In February the river reached its crest after rising three or four
feet daily. Now Patsy learned again what high water meant.
Now the Fosters were really up on top of the river bank. Their
whole point of view was so changed, it was hard to remember
how it used to be so far down below in the summer. Now the
houseboat seemed to be set in the middle of a great vast shallow
lake stretching as far as eye could see.

"I want it to get still higher," said Patsy, "so we can boatride
all around over the fields."

One day Patsy and Dan started out to explore in their own
red rowboat. Daddy had mended the leaks and made it service-
able. But the ride was not as much fun as they had thought it
would be. The river road to Tomato was entirely under water.

All the cotton fields were lakes now. The people in the houses were safe because their homes were set up high on stilts, but there were completely cut off and isolated. They could not use cars or trucks, but had to travel by boat.

"What will they do if the river comes up over their floor?" asked Patsy.

"They'll have to get in their boats and go somewhere else," said Dan, "somewhere over on the other side of the levee."

Maybe living in a house was not so desirable after all. Patsy thought about Grace Eva and Brenda Collins and the other children up the road. What about the Dillard boys and the Harris kids? How were they going to get to school? The school bus had stopped coming to the store corner. It came only as far as the levee now, and the levee was a whole mile inland, due to changes in the course of the river.

"We'll all just have to stay home from school till the river goes down," said Dan philosophically.

"But I *like* school," said Patsy. "I don't *want* to stay home."

"Maybe Daddy will take us in the johnboat," said Dan.

When they returned to the houseboat, they found that Daddy had tied it up to the big old sycamore tree right by his Fish Dock sign. The houseboat now sat in the middle of what had been the river road. It was only a stone's throw over to the Harrises' store. Patsy waved from her porch to Joella on hers, but the girls could not get together except by boat.

Patsy asked Daddy about the houses up the river road. "Is the river goin' to wash them away? They can't go up and down with the water the way we do."

[171]

Daddy laughed. "You think a houseboat's pretty nice now, don't you, honey? Well, those houses have been there a long time and I reckon they'll stay a little longer. When the river gets so high, all of a sudden it can't go higher and then it will start goin' down again.

"But how will we ever get to the school bus?" asked Patsy.

"The water's too deep to wade," said Dan. "I tried it."

"You *would*," said Mama.

Daddy answered Patsy's question by getting out the johnboat on the next school day and starting the motor. He made trips back and forth across the flooded cotton fields, carrying the river children over to meet the school bus and bringing them home again at night.

Spring came, a very wet spring. On April fifth, the river gauge was thirty-five feet. "That's the crest, I think," said Daddy. "Now it will start going down again. I got to be ready to catch the drop just right, if we're goin' to beach the houseboat."

Patsy clapped her hands. "Are we going to beach it and stay on land?"

"Ask your mama," said Daddy.

Yes, it was true. Mama had decided she had had enough of the river for a while and she wanted a change.

"I'm tired of the river," said Mama. "I'm tired of all this mud and of wading to this boat. Seems like I just got to get on dry land for a while or go crazy. We'll try it for the summer anyway and see how we like it."

"The mosquitoes will be bad," warned Daddy, "and it'll be hot as the dickens up here on the bank, without the river breeze."

"We'll try it anyhow," said Mama.

"You'll be glad to get back on the river again in a few months," said Daddy.

"Yes, I know," said Mama. "I'm as bad as you. When I quit goin' to the river, I'll be dead."

So Big Abe Foster asked George Milburn if he could beach. When he came back, he reported, "Mister George says the spot is ours and we can do what we want. He sure is nice to us—and there's no rent to pay."

When the water was just right, Daddy swung the houseboat around to the location he had chosen—off the road, at the brow of the hill, under the trees and beside a level stretch for clothes-line and a garden. He cut blocks three feet long and eight inches thick and put three under side of the houseboat, fastened them

to the hull and let the water go out from under it until the house-boat was resting on the blocks. When the water left, he jacked it up and leveled it off.

"It's a house now!" cried Patsy, delighted. "It's not a boat any more."

"We'll have to wait for another high water to move from this spot," said Daddy.

"A whole year in a house on land!" cried Patsy.

"That sounds terrible," said Daddy, "but you and your mother have been pestering me so . . . You're goin' to die of the heat in summer."

"No, the breeze from the river can hit us up here on the hill better than down under the river bank," said Mama. "The trees will keep the hot sun off the roof of the houseboat and it won't get so hot inside. We'll have to carry our wash water *up* hill instead of *down* . . ."

Everything seemed topsy-turvy for a time, but the Fosters were accustomed to change and soon got used to it.

"Daddy can go out fishing as well from here as from down below," said Mama, "and if it ever dries off, we'll be out of the mud."

"Gee," said Milly, "I wish summer would come!"

"So you can all go in swimming like ducks," said Mama. "Daddy can take the fish barge and the cabin boat and all the little boats down the hill as the water goes down, but as for me, I'm stayin' up here high and dry."

The river went down as fast as it had come up. As soon as the ground around the houseboat dried off, Patsy begged for a garden. Mr. George sent a man with a tractor to plow up the ground and Daddy helped her plant her seeds. She found two old discarded automobile tires for flower beds. In them she planted the geraniums that Aunt Edie had given her the fall before.

One thing led to another, and Daddy began to complain when he had to forego fishing for housepainting. But Mama was determined.

"A houseboat gets shabby if it's not kept painted," she said. "It can get to lookin' old mighty quick. We've got to keep it up. After all, it's our home."

Daddy put a coat of white on the house part and painted the hull a deep red. While he worked, Mama and Milly did a house cleaning inside. One day Andy Dillard, who was a good friend now, came up. Mama had washed and starched her curtains and was putting them on stretchers in the front yard.

"What you workin' up such a storm for?" asked Andy.

"I'm just stretchin' my curtains," said Mama.

"What! Worryin' and fussin' over curtains for a houseboat?" asked Andy.

"Why not?" answered Mama.

"We've got a big two-story house," said Dillard, "but there's not a single curtain in it."

"Well, I reckon I'm just fussy," said Mama. "I like my curtains and I like my quilts. It takes things like that to make a houseboat a home."

Now the Fosters lived in a different world, beside a busy country road. Cotton was being planted again in fields enriched by river soil deposits, and trucks and cars passed daily. At night they could see the lights in the store and lights in houses up the road, and the headlights of cars passing by. It was *almost* like living in town. But across the chute, Fork-a-Deer Island remained the same, unchanged, a wilderness tangle of brush and trees coming out in bud and leaf, a haven for animals, insects and birds of all kinds. Sitting on the porch on the leather couch, Daddy could look through the willows and feast his eyes on the island wilderness and on his beloved river below.

There was no river bank to climb now and Mama's clothesline was tied to one of the porch posts. All of Patsy's hens were gone but one and she was happy when Mrs. Cackle hatched out a brood of twenty new baby chicks. On the first really warm spring day, Mama washed four of her quilts, a Dutch Boy, a Nine Patch, a Flower Garden and a Crazy Quilt. They made a gay pattern of color under the trees, a true harbinger of spring.

Soon Joella and Brenda and Grace Eva came over to spend the night. Patsy slept with Brenda on the floor, while Joella and Grace Eva slept in the bunk beds. Milly was visiting a friend over night.

"It's not a houseboat any more," said Joella.

"No, it's a house," said Patsy. "It's my home!"

THE END